# THE
# BEATRIX POTTER

## $\mathcal{N}$EEDLEPOINT
## $\mathcal{B}$OOK

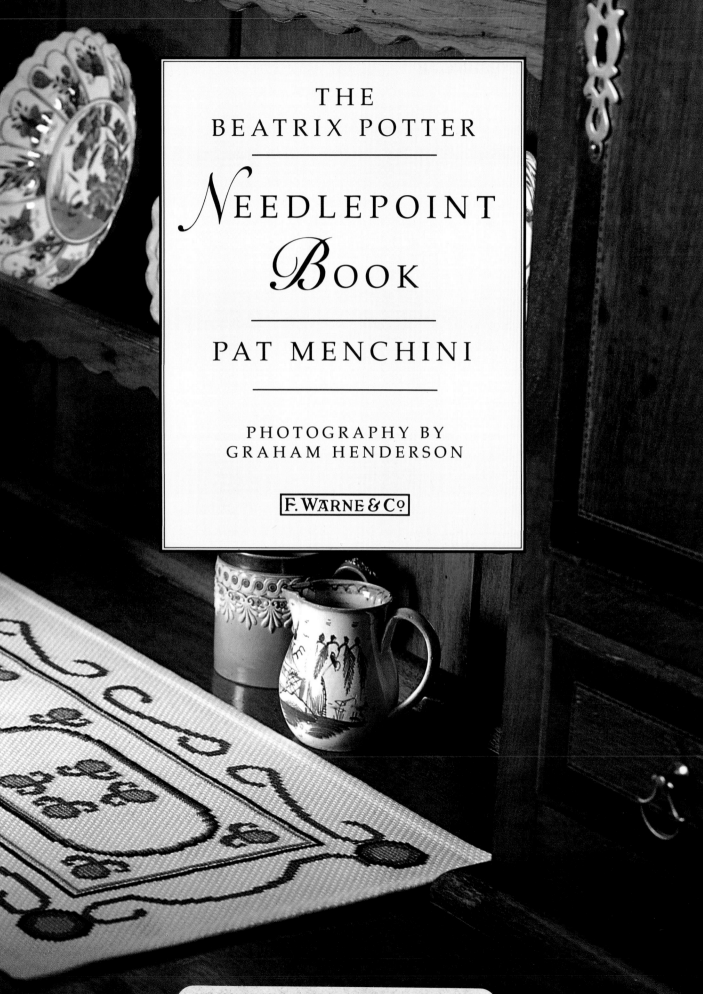

# THE
# BEATRIX POTTER

# NEEDLEPOINT
# BOOK

## PAT MENCHINI

PHOTOGRAPHY BY
GRAHAM HENDERSON

F. WARNE & Co.

FREDERICK WARNE

Published by the Penguin Group
27 Wrights Lane, London W8 5TZ, England
Penguin Books USA Inc., 375 Hudson Street, New York, New York 10014, USA
Penguin Books Australia Ltd, Ringwood, Victoria, Australia
Penguin Books Canada Ltd, 2801 John Street, Markham, Ontario, Canada L3R 1B4
Penguin Books (NZ) Ltd, 182–190 Wairau Road, Auckland 10, New Zealand

Penguin Books Ltd, Registered Offices: Harmondsworth, Middlesex, England

First published 1990
1 3 5 7 9 10 8 6 4 2

ISBN 0 7232 3663 1

Design by Ronnie Wilkinson
Charts by Raymond and Helena Turvey

Typeset, printed and bound in Great Britain by William Clowes Limited,
Beccles and London

The author and publishers would like to thank the following for their assistance:

*Taggart Studios* for all stretching, framing and upholstery, also picture stand for the mouse needlepoint. *Laura Ashley* for the
'Firenze' and 'Oleander' cotton fabric for the bedspread and tablecloth, also pillowcases. *Happicraft*, Wellingborough, for
embroidery fabrics and card mounts. *Buckden Antiques* for the tapestry frame. *Sue Terry* for the Victorian sewing box,
antique sewing accessories and lace for the heartsease design. *Bill Wallis, Irene Lazenby* and *Mr* and *Mrs Miles* for armfuls of
geraniums, white chrysanthemums, roses, heartsease and miniature flowers. *Bill Wallis*, too, for a wonderful old wooden
wheelbarrow and other gardening bygones. *Barbara Phillips* for the oak stool in the pansy design and lace cradle sheet.

The photograph of the costume on page 51 is reproduced by courtesy of the Trustees of the V & A Museum.

## ACKNOWLEDGEMENTS

My warmest thanks first of all, go to Graham Henderson, whose photography has captured so wonderfully the world of
Beatrix Potter. His clever and imaginative ideas truly evoke the spirit of life in Lakeland. Thank you, Graham, for your
patience as well!
I also wish to thank the National Trust for allowing us to photograph in Hill Top, Beatrix Potter's beloved old farmstead
at Near Sawrey, Cumbria. Special acknowledgement must go to Jill and Bill Latham who helped us so much at Hill Top. My
grateful thanks, too, to Dr and Mrs Kellgren, Janet and Chris Benefield and farmers George and Norman for the use of their
beautiful homes.
My uncle, Ron Adams, who gave great help and encouragement throughout, also stitched *twice* the landscape I designed
from an old photograph of his and I want to thank him again for the months of beautiful stitching he undertook for me.
Thanks, too, to Audrey Lane of Happicraft, Wellingborough, whose unending expert supply of information and materials
helped enormously with producing the designs.
This book would not have been possible without the help of all the yarn and thread manufacturers listed on page 126.
However, particular thanks for their help and patience must go to Alison Blair, Jessie Weir, Helen Cooper, Queenie Frisby,
Michael Kemp, Sandra Cook and Jane Ogden, and also to all the nimble-fingered needlepointers and knitters who have
worked away for me over the months, many of whom I have never met. I particularly wish to thank Gill Martyn, Jenny
Lacock and Hanne McDonald, who produced last-minute designs for me under great pressure!
Finally, I wish to thank my publisher, Sally Floyer, for her unfailing trust in me to carry through this huge project in an
unfamiliar field, and also to Ronnie Wilkinson for her superb book design.
PAT MENCHINI

# CONTENTS

# CONTENTS CONTINUED

*For my dear brother, Peter, my uncle Ron and my cousin Alan – three enthusiastic
needlepointers in my family – and, as always, for my patient, loving husband and two
dear daughters*

# INTRODUCTION

When I was asked to consider writing this book, following the publication of *The Beatrix Potter Knitting Book*, I must admit to having been rather overwhelmed by the idea! Not that I wasn't delighted to be considered for this huge and exciting task, but because I was not, and still do not consider myself, an embroidery designer, and some of the more elaborate techniques and materials which form part of this wide-ranging craft were unknown to me.

However, I was eventually convinced by those around me who knew my work and my capabilities, that I really should undertake the project. Certainly, the thought of being again in intimate touch with Beatrix Potter's art and the nostalgia and inspiration that her work invokes, drew me like a magnet. Rediscovering the Lakeland life and countryside as she knew them very soon swept aside any misgivings I might have had, and suddenly a great feeling of excitement and adventure came over me. Before I knew where I was, the designs were under way!

What appealed to me most initially was the access I would have to much of Beatrix Potter's little-known work, some of it indeed still unpublished. For only recently have certain pieces become available to the public, pieces which show her tremendous talent for absorbing colour and detail in subjects as varied as boats in the West Country and close-up studies of butterfly wings. The choice was enormous and thrilling! The other aspect which appealed to me greatly was the chance to express myself in the field of home interiors. Interior design has always held a great attraction for me, as it must have done for Beatrix Potter. She has left many drawings of furniture, fireplaces, rugs, cushions, shawls and plaids, taken from cottage homes in Lakeland, with their solid, country simplicity, or from stately houses like Melford Hall. And we know of her interest in country fairs and auctions, for she bought many small and large objects from such sources for her beloved first home in the Lake District, Hill Top.

I was particularly keen to co-ordinate a range of designs and this is why I also included certain knitted items to complement some of the needlepoints. I also wanted to encourage the use of embroidery for more unusual items, such as the pelmet and tie-back. Apart from that, being a knitting designer first and foremost, I could not resist the temptation to bring some knitting into the book – I loved mixing the different textures.

We photographed almost the entire book in the Lake District and much of it in Hill Top. You will be fascinated to see the dresser adorned with a cross-stitch runner in colours which exactly complement Beatrix's blue-and-white china. The Sad Rabbit cushion and the Cottage Afghan look so right on her rocking chair beside the famous kitchen fireplace featured in *The Tale of Tom Kitten*. I hope you enjoy spotting other Hill Top locations in the book too.

It is marvellous that Beatrix Potter continues to gain popularity more than 120 years after her birth. Enthusiasm increases as more of her beautiful legacy unfolds before the public eye. My own personal fascination with her work is still gaining momentum since my aunt bought me my first little books at the age of four. This fascination with her work and life upheld and inspired me whilst writing this book. However humble, compared with the genius of their original creator, I hope the designs will nevertheless encourage you to take up needle and thread and produce beautiful, hand-made and long-lasting pieces of work. Perfection is not vital, but colour and design and the pure pleasure of creating in today's busy, automated life, are. The preservation of all things natural, beautiful and unspoilt by mechanization is as important now as in Beatrix Potter's time, and this book is my contribution to such an aim. I hope you will enjoy the book for many years to come.

PAT MENCHINI

We strongly recommend firstly that a suitable frame is used: square or oblong for canvas, and round for fabrics.

The edging of the canvas should be covered in masking tape, and fabrics should be oversewn. For canvas and even-weave fabrics a tapestry needle with a rounded end must be used. Never use lengths of yarn in the needle over 43 cm/17 in long. On canvas work, every stitch should be worked in two movements, passing the needle back and forth from front to back. Try to work at an even tension and do not pull the threads too tightly. Keep the back of your work as smooth as possible and free from knots. Each time finish off by running the end of yarn neatly under a few stitches on the wrong side. We also recommend that large quantities of yarns, such as background colours, are purchased at the same time to avoid dye variations.

By commencing at the centre of a canvas and working outwards, you avoid possible stretching and bubbling of the work. Also in this way you can be sure to have the design correctly centred on the canvas. A canvas may need stretching if it has pulled slightly out of shape during work. *Do not* trim or mount the canvas until stretching is complete; this can be done professionally, but the following method may be undertaken at home. It is possible to stretch the canvas threads into their original shape by dampening the back and surrounding area to soften the stiffening agent, as described below. The moisture dries and resets the canvas threads. The canvas is left to dry naturally until the shape becomes permanent. This can take as long as 2 or 3 weeks. Cover a firm board slightly larger than the finished work with graph paper and draw an outline shape on the paper 5 cm/2 in larger than the embroidered tapestry. Now cut blotting paper to the size of the embroidered part and place on top of the graph paper to absorb moisture when dampening the tapestry (Fig. 1).

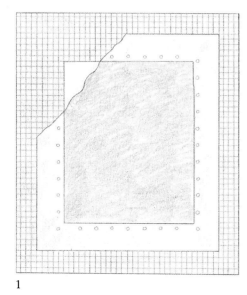

1

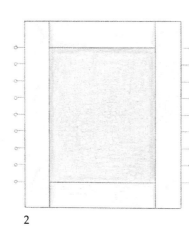

2

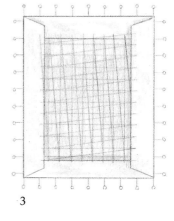

3

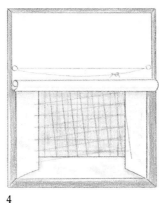

4

Fig. 1: *blocking and stretching the needle-point* Figs. 2, 3 *and* 4: *mounting canvas on a backing board, lacing across the wrong side to secure*

Using rustless drawing pins, pin out the canvas to size face downwards, making sure that warp and weft threads run at right angles to each other. Only if necessary, slightly dampen the worked canvas with a very light spray or moist rag. Using the outline on graph paper as a guide, secure round all edges of the unworked canvas, placing drawing pins 6 mm apart, parallel to outline. The canvas may require careful pulling in order to make it square. Remove pins. If necessary a second blocking and stretching may be required.

Keep needlepoint flat or carefully rolled up until

*Choosing a frame for the* Lakeland Landscape *needlepoint picture*

required. It may be mounted on a backing board as shown in Figs. 2, 3 and 4. Place the embroidery centrally over the backing board, fold surplus canvas to the back and secure at the top with pins into the edge of the board. Pull firmly over the lower edge and pin in position. Repeat for the side edges, pulling the canvas until it lies taut over the board. Secure at the back by lacing across both ways with stout thread; remove pins and place in frame.

# SOME USEFUL STITCHES AND TECHNIQUES

**HALF CROSS STITCH** on double
thread canvas

**HALF CROSS STITCH** on single
thread canvas

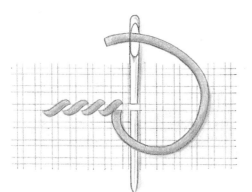

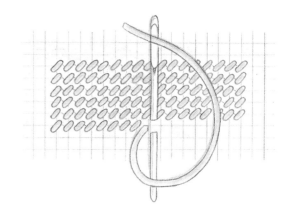

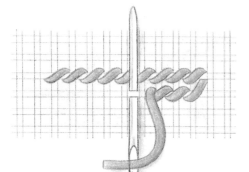

**CROSS STITCH** on Aida

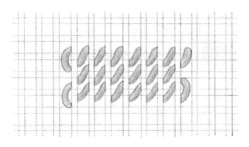

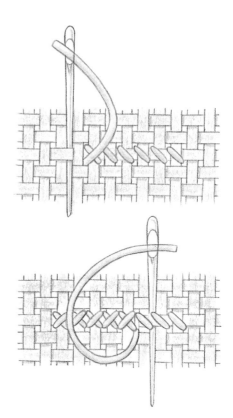

**CROSS STITCH** over 1

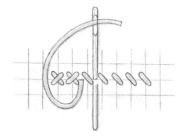

## TRAMMED GROS POINT STITCH

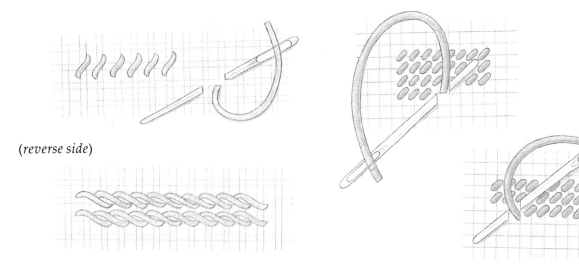

(*reverse side*)

To work a trammed stitch, the strand of yarn is brought through the double thread canvas at the intersection of a pair of vertical threads and a pair of horizontal threads. It is carried along the required distance (no longer than 13 cm/5 in) and passed back through the canvas at a similar intersection of threads. The gros point stitch is worked over the trammed stitch as shown in the diagram.

## CONTINENTAL TENT STITCH

The rows are worked from right to left and vice versa. Rows may also be worked diagonally. Bring thread out at the right-hand side, work a stitch diagonally upwards over one canvas thread interception, pass the needle diagonally downwards and bring through in readiness for next stitch. The second row is worked from left to right, the direction of the stitches is the same as the previous row but the needle is passed diagonally upwards.

## SATIN STITCH

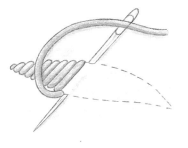

Work straight stitches closely together across the shape, as shown in the diagram. If desired, running stitch or chain stitch may be worked first to form a padding underneath. Do not make stitches too long, otherwise they may be pulled out of position.

## LONG AND SHORT STITCH

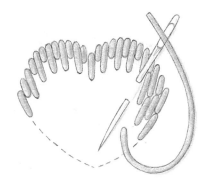

With this form of satin stitch, all the stitches are of varying lengths. It is therefore useful for filling in a shape which may be too large or too irregular to fill by using the simple method of satin stitch described on the left.

## STEM STITCH

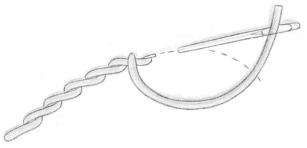

## STRAIGHT STITCH

## LONG STITCH

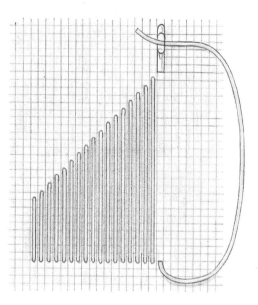

## FRENCH KNOTS

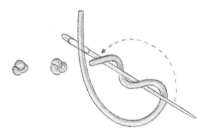

Bring yarn out to the required position, hold yarn down with left thumb and encircle it twice with the needle, as shown in the diagram. Still holding yarn firmly, twist the needle back to the starting point and insert it close to where the yarn first emerged (see arrow). Pull yarn through to back.

*Beatrix Potter's sewing mice, drawn for her first version of* The Tailor of Gloucester

## RUG-KNOTTING, METHOD 1

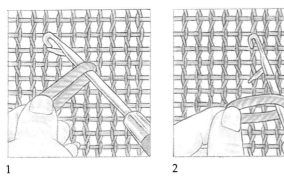

1                                    2

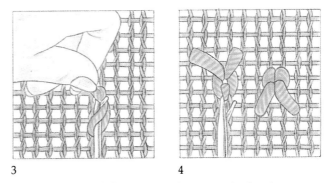

3                                    4

**1** Fold one piece of wool exactly in half round the shank of the hook; the evenness of the pile depends on this precise fold.

**2** Push the hook under the strands of canvas (weft) where the knot is to be made.

**3** Push the hook forward and ensure the latch is free to open, and turn the hook slightly to the right.

**4** Pull the hook through the loop of wool and push hook forward. Gently pull the two ends of the wool to make the knot firm.

## RUG-KNOTTING, METHOD 2

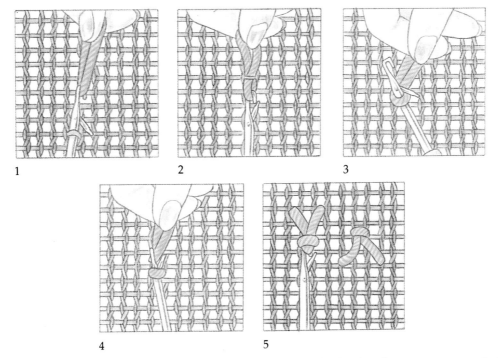

1                     2                     3

4                     5

**1** Push the hook under the strand of canvas (weft) where the knot is to be made until the latch lies behind the canvas. Fold one piece of wool in half and place this in the hook, ensuring the two ends are exactly the same length.

**2** Pull the hook back towards you so that about a third of the wool is in front and two thirds behind the canvas weft threads.

**3** Ensure the latch is free and open and place the free ends of the wool through the hook. Then allow the latch to close over the wool.

**4** Place the free ends of the wool through the hook and let the latch close.

**5** Pull the hook backwards and gently pull the knot to make it firm.

There are two methods of working cross stitch: with the row-by-row method, work a few half crosses, and then, starting with the last stitch, work back along the line – thus completing the second half of each cross stitch. With the stitch-by-stitch method, work each cross stitch individually.

The stitch-by-stitch method is preferable for small areas of stitching where only a few stitches are likely to be worked in any one colour. The row-by-row method is often used to cover large areas, such as the background. It is quicker to work and easier for maintaining an even tension, which is important.

It is essential with either method to ensure that all the stitches lie in the same direction.

ROW-BY-ROW METHOD

1 It is advisable to use lengths of wool no longer than 51 cm/20 in to prevent wool wearing thin during work.

2 To start stitching, leave a long horizontal thread under the row of canvas you are about to work. This avoids knots which may work through the canvas.

3 By bringing the needle up at the lower left-hand hole of the stitch to be worked and inserting it down through next diagonal hole, and repeating, half of each stitch is completed.

4 When all the half crosses for the intended area

have been worked, bring the needle up through the hole below and stitch back diagonally over the last stitch to complete the cross.

5 Working backwards, row by row, complete the second half of each cross stitch. Keep the tension as even as possible.

6 To fasten off thread on wrong side of work, slide needle through the back of 3 or 4 stitches, pull thread through and cut. There is no need to backstitch.

STITCH-BY-STITCH METHOD

1 An alternative method is to work each stitch individually. Work as steps 1 to 3 of the row-by-row method, but do not repeat step 3.

2 To complete the stitch, work back diagonally over the half cross worked previously and bring the needle up in the correct position for the next step. Fasten off as step 6 of the row-by-row method.

*Row-by-row method*

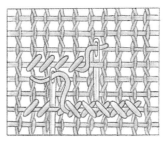

FRINGING

When adding a fringe to the ends of a rug, tie the tassels in the following order: starting from the left-hand end, take the first and third tassels, tie them together using an overhand knot and tighten this knot about 2 cm/1 in from end of rug. Next, take the second and fifth and knot together in the same way. Continue with the fourth and seventh, and so on until the row is completed. Trim evenly.

*Sequence for tying tassels*

## FINISHING A CIRCULAR RUG

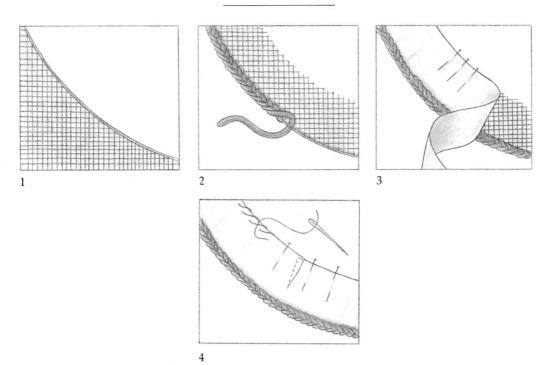

1

3

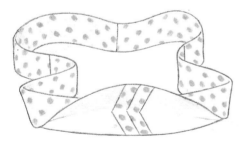

4

Finish working the rug and then cut away excess canvas approximately 5 cm/2 in from the edge of worked rug (Fig. 1). Turn back this canvas edge and work binding stitch along edge (Fig. 2). Pin carpet braid in position and stitch down outer edge (Fig. 3). Now stitch down inner edge, making darts as necessary to keep the braid flat (Fig. 4).

## SEWING A FRILL ON A CUSHION

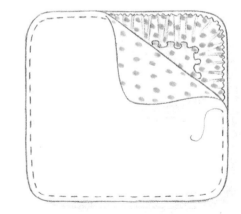

This method describes how to add a frill to a cushion such as the embroidered damask one on page 102.

Cut the frill fabric into 4 strips, cutting across width of the fabric. Sew strips together to form a ring. Press seams and fold in half lengthways, right side outside. Press fold. Gather up raw edges and stitch to damask, with raw edges of frill to raw edges of damask. Sew backing fabric to damask, right sides together, leaving a gap through which to insert pad. Turn cover inside out, insert pad and close seam.

## MR. JEREMY FISHER TEA COSY

---

*Mr. Jeremy Fisher's latticed window, surrounded
by buttercups, was the inspiration for the design
on this tea cosy. Trellis makes a lovely background
and is easy to work. I have tried to reflect the delicate,
watery feeling of the glass, highlighted by the bright
yellow flowers and vivid wings of Miss Butterfly
from* The Tale of Mrs. Tittlemouse. *The blues were
chosen to reflect the blue-and-white china
on the dresser at Hill Top.*

*From* The Tale of Mr. Jeremy Fisher

**NOTE**

The colours shown on the charts do not always
correspond with the colours of the yarns they
represent. This is to enable the different
shades to be identified more easily on
the charts.

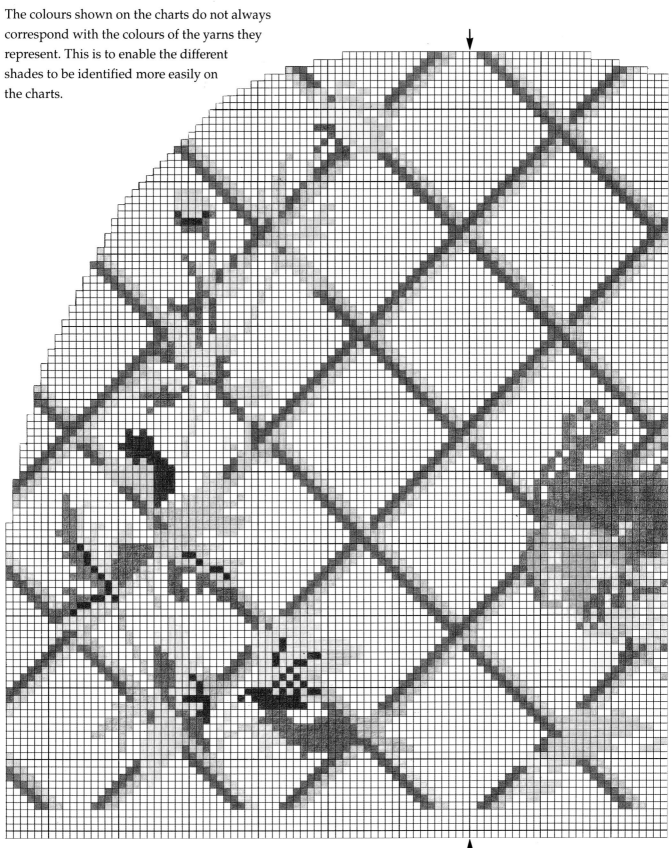

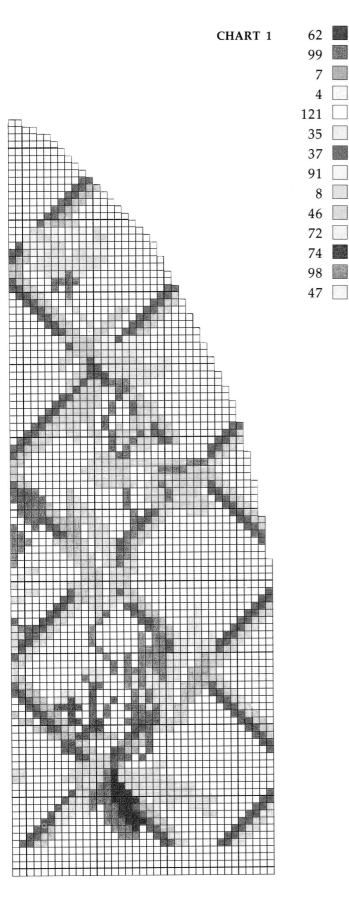

**CHART 1**

| | |
|---|---|
| 62 | ■ |
| 99 | ▨ |
| 7 | ▨ |
| 4 | ☐ |
| 121 | ☐ |
| 35 | ▨ |
| 37 | ▨ |
| 91 | ☐ |
| 8 | ▨ |
| 46 | ▨ |
| 72 | ▨ |
| 74 | ■ |
| 98 | ▨ |
| 47 | ☐ |

**MEASUREMENTS**

Finished cosy size: approximately 33 cm wide and 27 cm high/13 in wide and 10½ in high. N.B. An additional 5 rows have been allowed on chart for lower hem turning.

**MATERIALS**

**Twilley's Stranded Embroidery Wool** (12.5 g skeins)

5 skeins of colour 121, 2 skeins each of colours 35 and 37, and 1 skein each of colours 91, 8, 46, 72, 74, 98 and 47.

**Twilley's Lystra Stranded Cotton**

1 skein each of colours 62, 99, 7 and 4.

10-mesh double thread canvas, 2 pieces each 48 cm wide and 43 cm long/19 in wide and 17 in long. A size 20 tapestry needle. A length of lining fabric to measure 2 cm/1 in more all round than the 2 finished pieces of needlepoint. 1 metre length of cord. Matching sewing thread.

**TO MAKE**

The cosy is worked in 2 identical pieces. Follow chart 1 and use 2 strands of wool and 6 strands of cotton.

Work the entire canvas in trammed half cross stitch, following the instructions on pages 10 and 11 for preparing your canvas and blocking it.

Cut 2 pieces of lining fabric the size of the finished canvases plus 1.5 cm/⅝ in seam allowance round shaped edges.

With right sides together, backstitch the canvases to each other, and then stitch the lining pieces together, leaving lower edges free on each piece.

Trim seams on canvas and turn out to right side. Sew cord in position, making a loop at top. Turn under lower 5 rows of needlepoint and catch in position lightly.

Trim seam on lining. Insert lining into needlepoint, fold excess hem to inside and hem in position all round the lower (open) edges.

## SQUIRRELS ON A LOG

### FIRESCREEN

---

*The design of this firescreen is based on one of
Beatrix Potter's watercolour studies, with oak leaves
and acorns added to complement the picture.
This pair of squirrels may well have been the models
Beatrix Potter bought to perfect her drawings for
The Tale of Squirrel Nutkin. It is a highly complex
piece of needlepoint, as many of the colours are split
and re-blended, but I think the end result is well
worth the effort.
It might be interesting to try the outer border
in a darker neutral shade.*

*Squirrels on a log: one of Beatrix Potter's greetings card designs*

## CHART 2

| | | |
|---|---|---|
| 386 ☐ | 3041 ▦ | 615 ▨ |
| 398/378 ■ | 352 ▦ | 572/378 ▨ |
| 572 ▦ | 400 ▦ | 352/3041 ▨ |
| 3159 ☐ | 3025 ▨ | 572/400 ☐ |
| 397 ☐ | 402 ☐ | 3041/400 ■ |
| 398 ▦ | 403 ■ | 400/352 ▨ |
| 842 ☐ | 279 ☐ | 3159/397 ▦ |
| 266 ▦ | 280 ☐ | 3159/402 ▦ |
| 672 ▦ | 860 ☐ | 3159/572 ▦ |

### MEASUREMENTS

Finished tapestry size: 41 cm wide and 51 cm high/ 16 in wide and 20 in high.

### MATERIALS

**Anchor Tapisserie Wool**

9 skeins of colour 386, 2 skeins each of colours 378, 572, 3159, 397, 398, 842, 266, 672, then 1 skein each of colours 3041, 352, 400, 3025, 402, 403, 279, 280, 860 and 615.

10-mesh double thread canvas 56 cm wide and 66 cm long/22 in wide and 26 in long. A size 18 tapestry needle. Firescreen frame and backing board to fit (purchase on completion of embroidery).

### TO MAKE

Follow chart 2. Where the key shows 2 colours to be used together, separate the wool into 4 strands and use 2 strands of each colour in the needle at the same time. Work the entire canvas in half cross stitch.

Follow the instructions on pages 10 and 11 for preparing your canvas and blocking it.

Mark the centre of the canvas widthwise and lengthwise with a line of basting stitches. Commence the work at the centre and work outwards from this point.

To mount your finished picture, follow the instructions and diagrams on pages 10 and 11.

# SQUIRREL WITH NUT CUSHION

*This is one of my favourite pieces: I love the way the squirrel looks as though he is just about to dart*

*off (see the photograph on page 22). He actually comes from a sketchbook full of squirrels which*

*Beatrix Potter drew in 1903 as preparation for* The Tale of Squirrel Nutkin. *Again, I have added*

*oak leaves to the picture as Beatrix painted these so many times. Ivy leaves with berries are also*

*included (top left-hand corner), to add to the interest of the design.*

## MEASUREMENTS
Finished cushion size: approximately 44 × 34 cm/
17½ × 13½ in.

## MATERIALS
**Anchor Tapisserie Wool**
8 skeins of colour 3085, 3 of colour 397, 2 of colour
398, then 1 each of colours 572, 650, 3159, 400, 873,
403, 386, 859, 421, 279, 842, 860, 280, 266, 672, 615
and 378.
10-mesh double thread canvas 51 cm wide and
41 cm long/20 in wide and 16 in long. A size 18
tapestry needle. A cushion pad to fit. A piece of
backing fabric 53 × 43 cm/21 × 17 in. Braid. Matching sewing thread.

## TO MAKE
Follow chart 3. Work the entire canvas in half cross
stitch.
Follow instructions on pages 10 and 11 for preparing your canvas and blocking it.
Mark the centre of the canvas widthwise and
lengthwise with a line of basting stitches. Commence the work at centre and work outwards from
this point.

With right sides together, backstitch the canvas to
the backing fabric, leaving a gap through which to
insert the cushion pad. Trim seams and turn out to
right side. Insert pad and close the remaining seam.
Sew on braid.

*Left: Squirrel sketch by Beatrix Potter in pencil and watercolour*

## CHART 3

| | | | | |
|---|---|---|---|---|
| 3085 | ☐ | | 859 | ☐ |
| 397 | ☐ | | 421 | ☐ |
| 398 | ▨ | | 279 | ☐ |
| 572 | ☐ | | 842 | ☐ |
| 650 | ■ | | 860 | ▨ |
| 3159 | ☐ | | 280 | ☐ |
| 400 | ▨ | | 266 | ■ |
| 873 | ▨ | | 672 | ▨ |
| 403 | ■ | | 615 | ▨ |
| 386 | ☐ | | 378 | ■ |

# OAK LEAVES AND RIBBON RUG

## Tufted rug

---

*Oak leaves reappear on this delightful tufted rug, which perfectly complements the cushion and*

*firescreen (see the photograph on page 22). A garland of ribbon brings the design together.*

*Rug-making is easy to master, needing just a modicum of patience. The ideal occupation for long*

*winter evenings!*

**MEASUREMENTS**
Finished rug size: 69 × 137 cm/27 × 54 in.

**MATERIALS**
**Readicut Rug Wool** (320 pieces per pack)
45 packs of colour 36, 2 packs each of colours 53, 22,

16, 50, 13 and 60, then 1 pack each of colours 17, 95, 90, 76, 32 and 48.

$3\frac{1}{3}$-mesh interlock rug canvas 69 cm wide and 152 cm long/27 in wide and 60 in long. Latchet hook. Matching sewing thread.

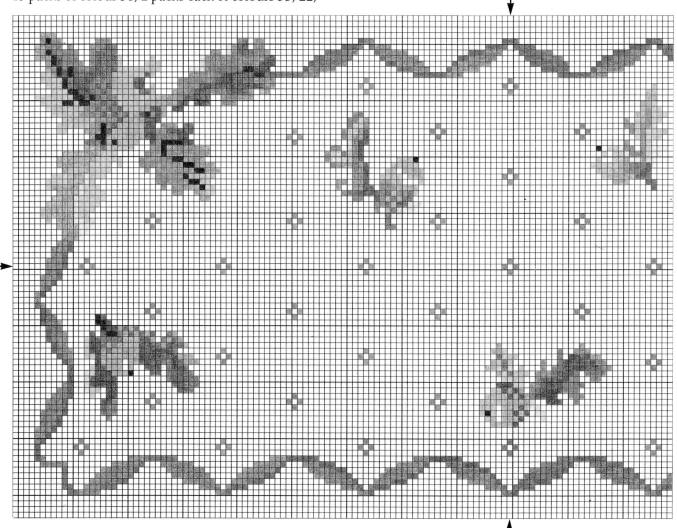

## RUG-MAKING AT HOME

Rug-making is most simple if you sit at a table with one end of the canvas facing you, so that the knots are worked on the line of canvas which lies on the edge of the table; a weight placed on the unworked canvas will help support the worked part of the rug.

## MAKING THE KNOT

The knots can be made by either Method 1 or Method 2, described on page 15. They are equally quick and the only difference is that the pile fabrics worked by the two methods lie in different directions. This can be turned to advantage so as to enable two people to work at the rug from opposite ends of the canvas towards the middle. If one person uses Method 1 and the other Method 2 all the completed pile will lie in the same direction.

## TO MAKE

Fold under 4 cm/1½ in of the canvas across the width of the starting edge and work through both thicknesses of canvas: this gives a strong finish. Always work in rows across the width of the canvas from selvedge to selvedge.

Knot through every stitch following chart 4 illustrated below. Do not work blocks of pattern or colours separately.

The last few rows are worked double in the same way as the starting edge.

Fold under the 2 selvedges and stitch neatly in position.

## RUG CARE AND CLEANING

Shake out loose dirt and vacuum clean both sides of the rug. With a cloth or brush moistened in liquid detergent, lightly clean the pile. If required, light hand-shampooing machines may be used. Dry by hanging the rug on a line away from direct sunlight or by laying it flat. The rug may be dry-cleaned professionally if desired.

Do not attach any backing material such as hessian, etc. Do not use a washing-machine or allow the rug to become soaking wet. Do not use heavy shampooing machines or tumble dry.

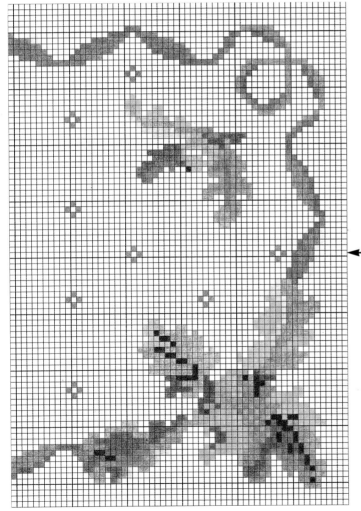

**CHART 4**

| | | | |
|---|---|---|---|
| 36 |  | 17 | 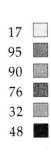 |
| 53 | | 95 | |
| 22 | | 90 | |
| 16 | | 76 | |
| 50 | | 32 | |
| 13 | | 48 | |
| 60 | | | |

# TOM KITTEN CUSHION

*Tom Kitten's look of wide-eyed innocence conceals a mischievous nature, as those familiar with his adventures will know. I created this design totally freehand, bringing in many subtle shades to recreate Tom's tabby coat and appealing expression, and was delighted with the result. Ferns, flowers and an impression of the dry-stone wall from* The Tale of Tom Kitten *make an attractive background.*

**MEASUREMENTS**
Finished cushion size: approximately 30 cm/12 in square.

**MATERIALS**
**Anchor Tapisserie Wool**
3 skeins each of colours 985 and 397, 2 skeins each of colours 713, 438 and 504, 1 skein each of colours 738, 711, 623, 702, 421, 498, 987, 386, 899, 313, 3485, 96, 97, 278, 3087 and 400.
10-mesh double thread canvas 46 cm/18 in square. A size 18 tapestry needle. A cushion pad to fit. A piece of backing fabric 36 cm/14 in square. Length of cord for edging cushion. Matching sewing thread.

**TO MAKE**
Following chart 5, work as given for the squirrel cushion on page 26.

*From* The Tale of Tom Kitten

31

# TOM KITTEN PICTURE

CHART 5

*Having finished the Tom Kitten cushion,*
*I thought a close-up of his face would be attractive –*
*and not just for the nursery (see photograph on page 34).*

**MEASUREMENTS**
Finished tapestry size: approximately 24 cm/9½ in square.

**MATERIALS**
**Anchor Tapisserie Wool**
2 skeins of colour 738, 1 skein each of colours 711, 623, 702, 421, 498, 713, 987, 985, 386, 899, 504 and 397.
10-mesh double thread canvas 41 cm/16 in square.
A size 18 tapestry needle. A picture frame with backing board to fit.

**TO MAKE**
Follow chart 5, working the square area outlined in black, and work in half cross stitch.
Follow the instructions on pages 10 and 11 for preparing your canvas and blocking it.
Mark the centre of the canvas widthwise and lengthwise with a line of basting stitches. This should correspond with the centre of the area of chart 5 to be worked.
When the main part of the canvas has been worked, add 1 row of 713 all round, followed by 5 rows of 738.

Mount your canvas on the backing board, following the instructions and diagrams on pages 10 and 11.

| Colour | |
|---|---|
| 738 | ☐ |
| 711 | ☐ |
| 623 | ▨ |
| 702 | ▨ |
| 421 | ▨ |
| 498 | ▨ |
| 713 | ▨ |
| 987 | ■ |
| 985 | ▨ |
| 386 | ☐ |
| 899 | ☐ |
| 504 | ☐ |
| 397 | ▨ |
| 96 | ▨ |
| 97 | ▨ |
| 278 | ▨ |
| 313 | ▨ |
| 400 | ▨ |
| 3087 | ▨ |
| 3485 | ▨ |
| 438 | ☐ |

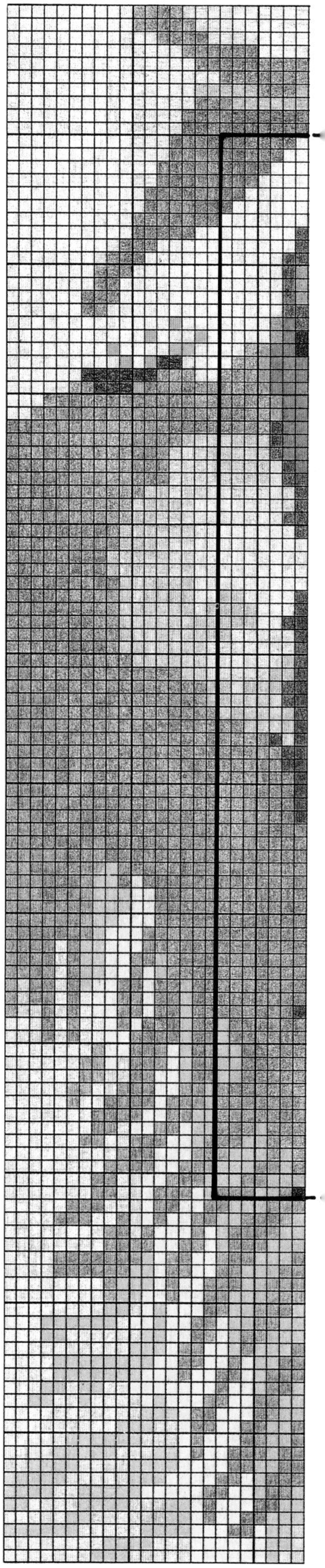

# PATCHWORK SHAWL

*The creams, blues and browns of Tom Kitten's cushion and picture are repeated in this cosy shawl: much quicker to make up than true patchwork, as the motif shapes are knitted in long strips and then stitched together.*

**MEASUREMENTS**
Finished shawl size: approximately 102 cm/40 in square after pressing.

**MATERIALS**
**Patons Pure Wool DK** (50 g balls)
3 balls each of Cream (A), Blue (B), Brown (C), Stone (D) and Grey (E).
A pair of 4½ mm/No 7 needles.

**TENSION**
Instructions are based on a standard garter-stitch tension of 19 sts and 38 rows to 10 cm/4 in on 4½ mm needles.

**ABBREVIATIONS**
K = knit; ml = make loop by wrapping yarn round right needle (i.e. empty needle); sts = stitches; rep = repeat.

**TO MAKE**
STRIP A (make 8)
With A, cast on 10 sts.
**1st to 12th rows:** In A, ml, k to end. (*22 sts*)
**13th row:** In A, ml, k2, slip 2, k1, pass 2 slipped sts over st just knitted, k to last 6 sts, k3 together, k3.
**14th row:** In A, ml, k to end.
**15th to 24th rows:** Rep 13th and 14th rows 5 times. (*10 sts*)
**25th to 120th rows:** Rep the last 24 rows 4 times more, working 24 rows B, 24 rows C, 24 rows D and 24 rows E.

*Opposite: The Tom Kitten picture and shawl with an old wooden wheelbarrow of the type shown in* The Tale of Peter Rabbit

Rep these 120 rows once, then rows 1 to 96 again. Cast off.

STRIP B (make 7)
With C, cast on 22 sts.
**1st to 12th rows:** In C, rep 13th and 14th rows of Strip A 6 times. (*10 sts*)
**13th to 108th rows:** Rep rows 1 to 24 of Strip A 4 times but working 24 rows in D, 24 rows E, 24 rows A, then 24 rows B.
**109th to 120th rows:** In C, work 1st to 12th rows of Strip A.
Keeping colour sequence correct, work 216 more rows. Cast off.

TO MAKE UP
Join strips together, alternating as you go, using D to link loop edge sts together with an oversewing stitch. Press following instructions on wool band.

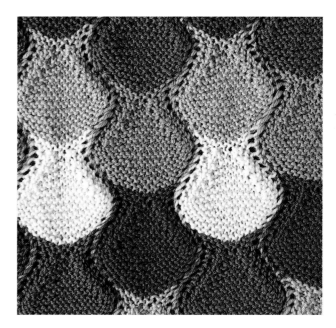

# FRUIT DESIGN PELMET,

## TIE-BACK AND CUSHIONS

---

*I found the glowing colours and composition of Beatrix Potter's various studies of fruit very inspiring, and created this design from six or seven of her paintings. The dark background adds a rich atmosphere and really emphasizes the fruit. Note Beatrix's little pet lizard, too! This was one of the most complicated pieces to do. I planned and drew the fruit freehand, and then another two or three weeks' work was needed to design the chart.*

**MEASUREMENTS**

Finished pelmet size: approximately 91 cm long and 18 cm high/36 in long and 7 in high. Finished tie-back size: approximately 46 cm long and 18 cm high at widest part/18 in long and 7 in high. Cushions: approximately 30 cm/12 in square.

**MATERIALS**

PELMET

**Anchor Tapisserie Wool**

6 skeins of colour 703, 4 skeins of colour 721, 2 skeins each of colours 402, 899, 3186, 373, 985, 3097, 3230, 3101, 3175, 626, 850, 3124, 3166, 412,

3152 and 3085, finally 1 skein each of colours 868, 218, 160, 123, 99, 148, 601, 64, 873, 869 and 280. 10-mesh double thread canvas 102 cm wide by 28 cm high/40 in wide by 11 in high. A size 18 tapestry needle. Backing board to fit finished needlepoint. Optional fringing for lower edge of pelmet and matching cord for other 3 edges. Matching sewing thread.

TIE-BACK

**Anchor Tapisserie Wool**

3 skeins of colour 703, then 1 skein each of colours 402, 899, 868, 3186, 373, 985, 3097, 3230, 721, 3101, 3175, 626, 218, 160, 850, 123, 99, 148, 601, 64, 3124, 3166, 412, 3152, 873, 3085, 869 and 280. 10-mesh double thread canvas 58 cm wide by 28 cm high/23 in wide by 11 in high. A size 18 tapestry needle. Backing fabric approximately 56 cm by 46 cm/22 in by 18 in. Length of cord for edging. Sewing thread to match background.

*A still life picture of grapes and peaches painted by Beatrix Potter in October 1883 when she was seventeen*

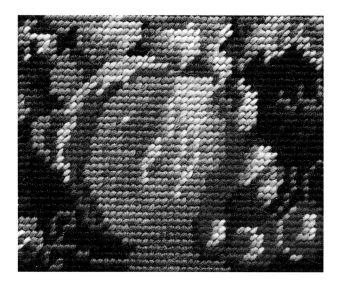

*Detail of cushion A*

*Detail of cushion B*

## CUSHION A (Peaches and Cherries)
**Anchor Tapisserie Wool**

4 skeins of colour 3072, 3 skeins of colour 703, 2 skeins of colour 721, 1 skein each of colours 402, 899, 868, 3186, 373, 985, 3097, 3230, 3101, 3175, 626, 218, 160, 850, 123, 99, 148, 64, 3124, 3166, 412, 3152 and 3085.

7-mesh double thread canvas 41 cm/16 in square. A size 18 tapestry needle. A piece of backing fabric 28 cm/11 in square. A cushion pad to fit. Cord for edging if desired. Matching sewing thread.

## CUSHION B (Raspberries and Plums)
**Anchor Tapisserie Wool**

4 skeins of colour 507, 3 skeins of colour 703, 2 skeins of colour 3186, 1 skein each of colours 402, 899, 868, 373, 985, 3230, 721, 3101, 3175, 626, 218, 160, 850, 123, 99, 601, 64, 3124, 3166, 412, 3152, 873, 3085, 869 and 280.

Remainder of materials as for Cushion A.

### TO MAKE PELMET

Follow chart 6 completely for right half, using tapisserie wool.

Work the entire canvas in half cross stitch. Work in reverse for left half of canvas – we are unable to show the second half in the book because of limited space.

Follow the instructions on pages 10 and 11 for preparing your canvas and blocking it.

Mark centre of each half of design widthwise and lengthwise. Commence work at centre point of right half.

Mount canvas on the backing board as described on page 11.

If desired, fringing may be pinned to lower edge and cord around the other 3 edges.

### TO MAKE TIE-BACK

Follow the relevant outlined section on chart 6.

Work the entire canvas in half cross stitch.

Follow the instructions on pages 10 and 11 for preparing your canvas and blocking it.

Mark centre widthwise and lengthwise. Commence work at centre point.

Cut 2 crossway pieces of fabric from a corner of the backing fabric, each 13 × 3 cm/5 × 1½ in, for loops. Stitch each piece lengthwise to form 2 tubes. Turn out. Folding each one in a loop and with loop facing towards centre of *right* side of canvas, tack in position to the 2 short ends of canvas.

Lay the backing fabric over the canvas with right sides together. Pin at right angles to the edge of embroidery and stitch all round with a fine back-stitch seam close to outer row of needlepoint, leaving a 10 cm/4 in gap through which to turn out. Trim seams. Turn out and close gap. Sew on cord.

CENTRE FOR PELMET

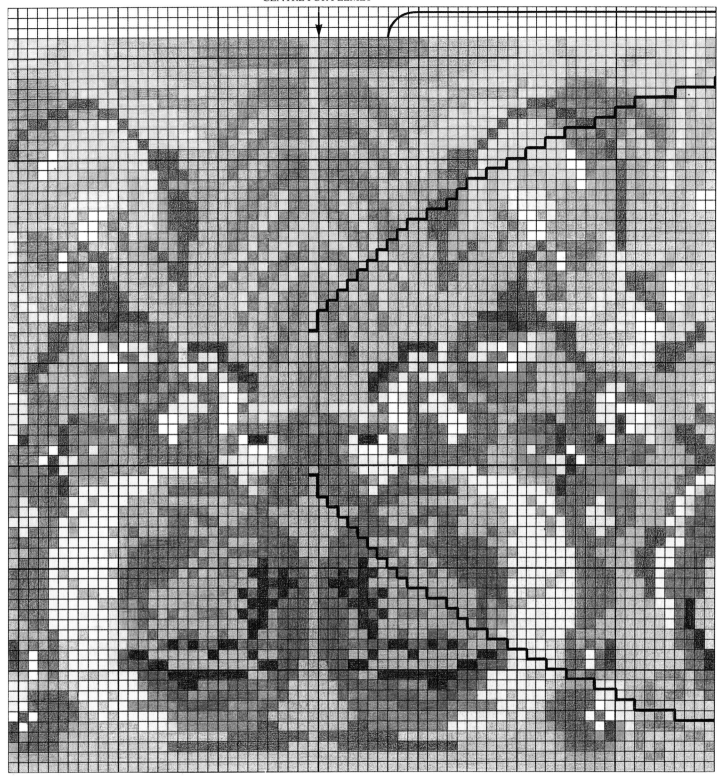

**CHART 6**

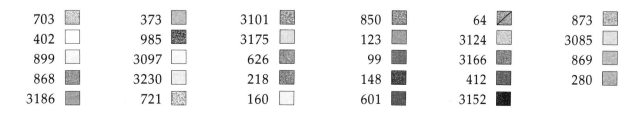

| | | | | | |
|---|---|---|---|---|---|
| 703 | 373 | 3101 | 850 | 64 | 873 |
| 402 | 985 | 3175 | 123 | 3124 | 3085 |
| 899 | 3097 | 626 | 99 | 3166 | 869 |
| 868 | 3230 | 218 | 148 | 412 | 280 |
| 3186 | 721 | 160 | 601 | 3152 | |

### TO MAKE CUSHION A

Follow the relevant outlined section on chart 6 but omit the lizard section, which should be worked in 703 using double thickness of wool throughout. Work the entire canvas in half cross stitch.

Follow the instructions on pages 10 and 11 for preparing your canvas and blocking it.
Mark the centre of the canvas widthwise and lengthwise. Commence work at centre point.
Finish needlepoint by working an 8-stitch border all

round in 3072, again using double wool.
Complete the cushion according to the instructions given for the squirrel cushion described on page 26. Cord may be stitched round edges if desired, to add a decorative effect.

## TO MAKE CUSHION B

Using 507 for border and omitting the lizard area, which should be worked instead in 703 (alternatively design a grape to fill the space!), work as given for Cushion A.

# HUNCA MUNCA FLOOR RUNNER

## Cross stitch

—————————

*Here, I have tried to recreate the rug in the doll's house from* The Tale of Two Bad Mice, *using the tiny piece shown in the very last picture of the book as a starting point. Both floor and table runners beautifully complement the Hill Top dresser, with its blue-and-white china. I had forgotten to measure up the dresser on an initial visit to Hill Top but, joy of joys, when we set the photograph up, the runner actually fitted the required area and the whole shot worked perfectly.*

**MEASUREMENTS**
Finished runner size: approximately 56 × 193 cm/ 22 × 76 in.

**MATERIALS**
**Paterna Persian Yarn** (4 oz hanks)
3 hanks of colour 500 (Dark Blue), 4 hanks of colour 502 (Medium Blue), 2 hanks of colour 504 (Light Blue) and 10 hanks of colour 262 (Cream – main shade).
5-mesh rug canvas 66 cm wide and 203 cm long/ 26 in wide and 80 in long. A size 13 bodkin needle. Matching sewing thread. Optional carpet braid.

**TO MAKE**
Follow chart 7. Mark the centre of the canvas widthwise and lengthwise with a line of basting stitches. Each square on the chart represents one intersection of the canvas.
Work the entire canvas in cross stitch, using 6 strands of yarn together. See the note 'Cross stitch for rugs' and the diagram on page 16.

*From* The Tale of Two Bad Mice

43

Chart 7 shows the upper left-hand quarter of the design. Begin at the *centre* of the rug and when the upper left-hand quarter has been completed, work the upper right-hand quarter to match. Turn the chart upside down and work the lower right-hand quarter, then work the lower left-hand quarter to match.

Finally, work 2 rows in 504, followed by 3 rows in 500 all round.

Trim away excess canvas, leaving about 5 squares free all round. Canvas edges may be lightly stitched down in place, or covered with carpet braid over the raw edges if desired.

**CHART 7**

| | |
|---|---|
| 500 ■ | 504 ▦ |
| 502 ▨ | 262 □ |

*In the picture above, from* The Tale of Samuel Whiskers, *Beatrix Potter has used the Hill Top dresser and its blue-and-white china as background*

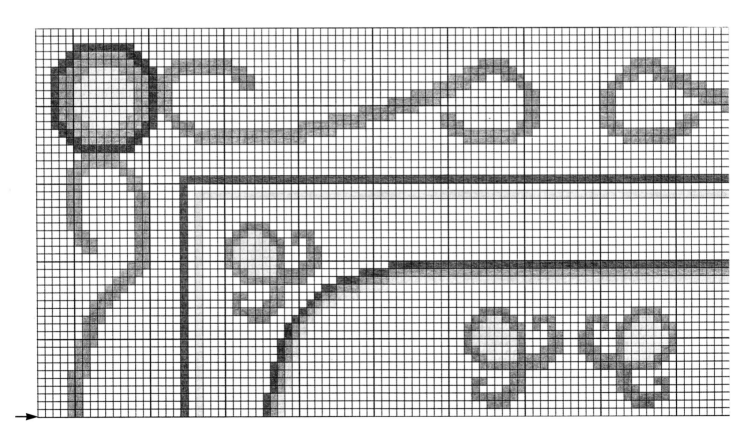

# HUNCA MUNCA TABLE RUNNER

## Cross stitch

---

**MEASUREMENTS**
Finished runner size: approximately 89 × 28 cm/
35 × 11 in.

**MATERIALS**
**Twilley's Lystra Stranded Cotton**
2 skeins of colour 87 (Dark Blue), 5 skeins of colour
92 (Medium Blue) and 3 skeins of colour 111 (Light
Blue).
11-mesh white Aida embroidery material 102 cm
wide and 38 cm long/40 in wide and 15 in long. A
size 18 tapestry needle. White sewing thread.

**TO MAKE**
Follow chart 7, using 3 strands of cotton throughout. Each square on the chart represents one
intersection on the Aida.

Overcast the raw edges to avoid fraying, then work
the entire embroidery in cross stitch. Mark the
centre of the material widthwise and lengthwise
with a line of basting stitches. Start from the centre
of the design and count outwards. All top stitches
must run in the same direction. Finish each length
by running it under a few stitches.
The chart shows the upper left-hand corner. When
this is worked, stitch the lower left-hand corner in
reverse. Work the remaining half of the embroidery
in reverse to match the first half.

Trim the embroidery to within approximately 5 cm/
2 in of the outer edge of embroidery along all 4
sides. Press under 3 squares, then a further 4
squares, and hem neatly all round. Press wrong side
of embroidery carefully under a damp cloth.

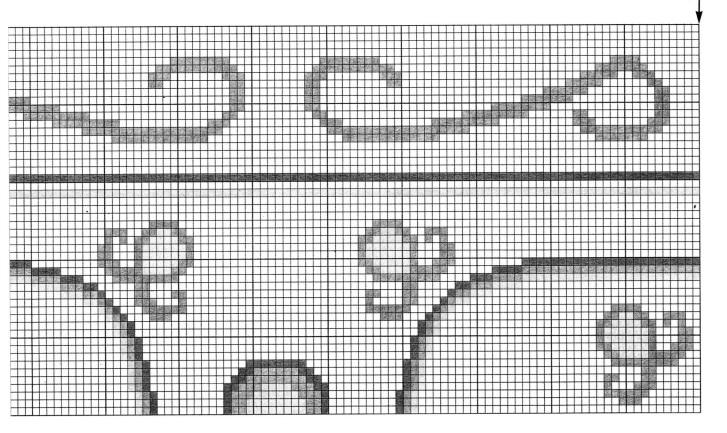

*The Hunca Munca table runner displayed on Beatrix Potter's own dresser at Hill Top*

# FLORAL STOOL COVER

*Beatrix Potter's grandfather, Edmund Potter, owned a large printing works near Manchester, and
she used some of his printed calico to make folders to hold her drawings. I loved the little Victorian
prints straight away, and came up with this simplified version of one of them. It is ideal for a
beginner, and the small pattern repeat makes it suitable for all sorts of articles. Many different
colour combinations can be tried; I chose blues in this instance to match the floor runner.*

**MEASUREMENTS**

Finished stool cover size: approximately 37 ×
32 cm/14½ × 12½ in.
NB: The cover is worked from a small chart
repeated to fit size required. This design is therefore
suitable for many upholstered articles.

**MATERIALS**

**Paterna Persian Yarn** (8 yd skeins)
16 skeins of colour 506, 4 skeins of colour 531, 3
skeins each of colours 504 and 532 and 2 skeins of
colour 502.
10-mesh interlock canvas 51 cm wide and 46 cm
long/20 in wide and 18 in long. A size 18 tapestry
needle. Stool to fit. Fringed braid if desired.

*Above: Fabric samples from Beatrix Potter's grandfather's
printing works*

**TO MAKE**

Follow the instructions on pages 10 and 11 for
preparing your canvas and blocking it.
Mark the canvas widthwise and lengthwise with a
line of tacking stitches.
Starting at centre of design, lining up arrows to
match tacking on the canvas, work chart 25 in half
cross stitch. Now work outwards from centre until
work measures 37 × 32 cm/14½ × 12½ in, or desired
size.

**CHART 25**

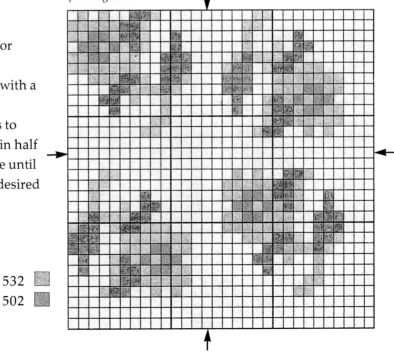

| | | | |
|---|---|---|---|
| 506 | ☐ | 532 | ▨ |
| 531 | ▨ | 502 | ▨ |
| 504 | ▨ | | |

49

# TAILOR OF GLOUCESTER

## UPHOLSTERED CHAIR SEAT

---

*I just had to bring into this book the exquisite embroidered coat and waistcoat from* The Tailor of Gloucester, *who 'sewed and snippeted all day long while the light lasted'. Beatrix Potter, in turn, copied details from eighteenth-century clothes in the Victoria and Albert Museum for her painting, so this embroidery is steeped in history. A fine piece of work.*
*I must include a huge thank-you to the lady who stitched the design for me. She had almost finished when her house was burgled and the canvas taken, and the poor thing had to start right again from scratch.*

**MEASUREMENTS**
The top area of the chair seat measures 36 cm deep by 38 cm wide/14 in deep by 15 in wide at the widest point. In addition, the chart allows for a further 4 cm/1½ in all round. You will need to consult your upholsterer to ensure that sufficient worked canvas is allowed for edges.

**MATERIALS**
**Anchor Tapisserie Wool**
24 skeins of colour 384, 5 skeins of colour 69, 2 skeins each of colours 67, 3197, 712, 736 and 503, then 1 skein each of colours 215, 188, 432, 700, 3230, 402 and 635.
10-mesh double thread canvas 61 cm/24 in square.
A size 18 tapestry needle.

**TO MAKE**
Follow chart 9, working the entire canvas in trammed gros point.
Follow the instructions on pages 10 and 11 for

*The photograph on the right shows the eighteenth-century waistcoat which Beatrix Potter discovered on display at the Victoria and Albert Museum and which she copied for* The Tailor of Gloucester

preparing your canvas and blocking it.
Mark centre of canvas widthwise and lengthwise with a line of basting stitches. Commence the work at centre. When centre is complete, work the trellis lines and rosebuds. Finally, fill in background.

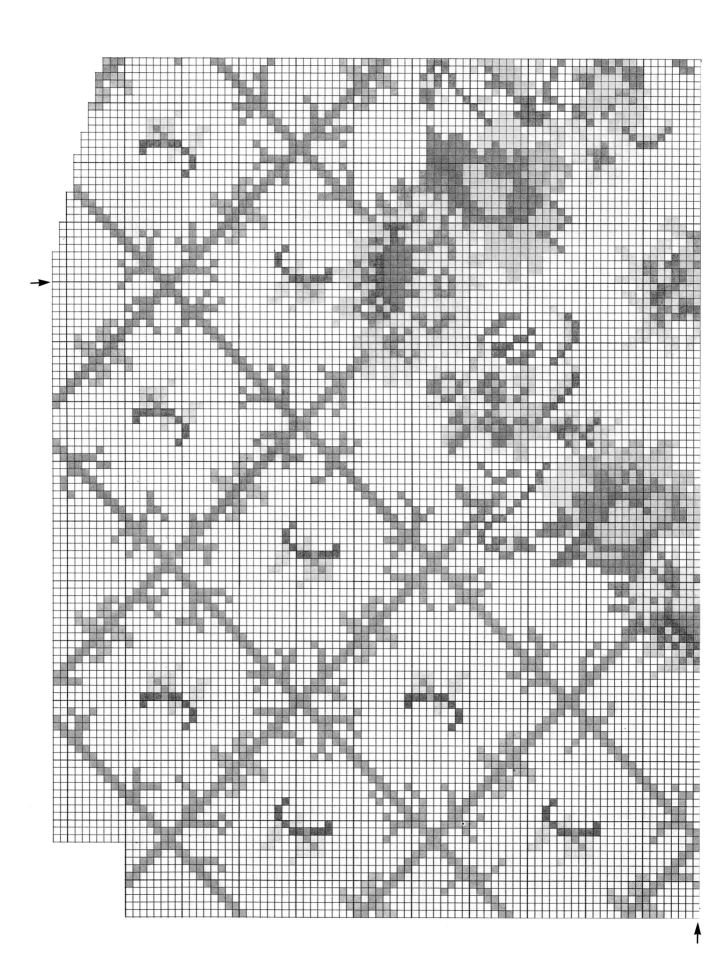

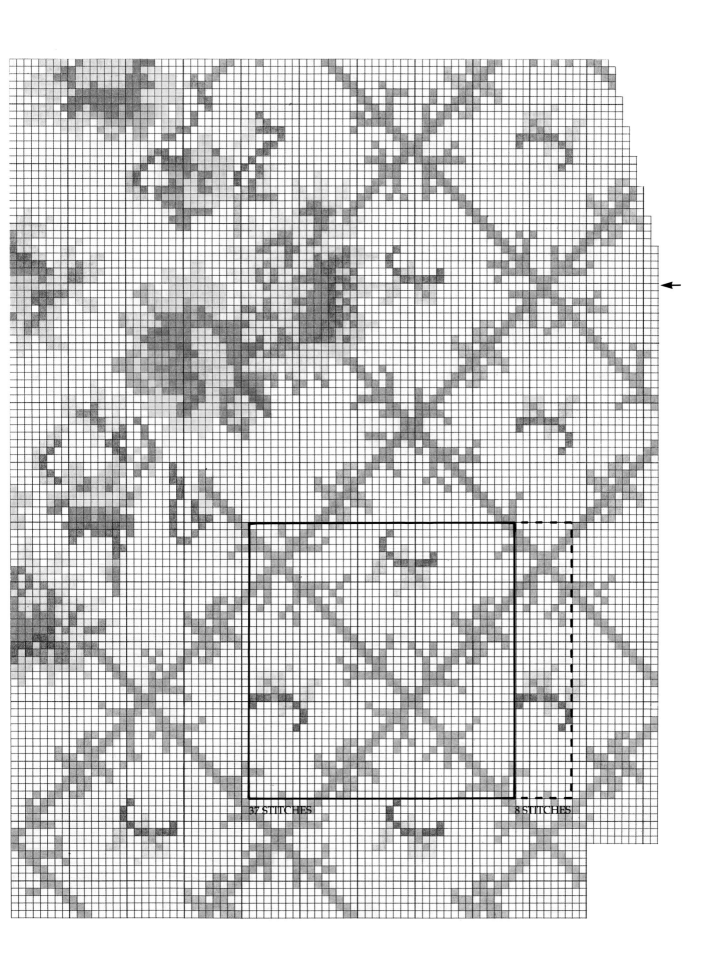

37 STITCHES

8 STITCHES

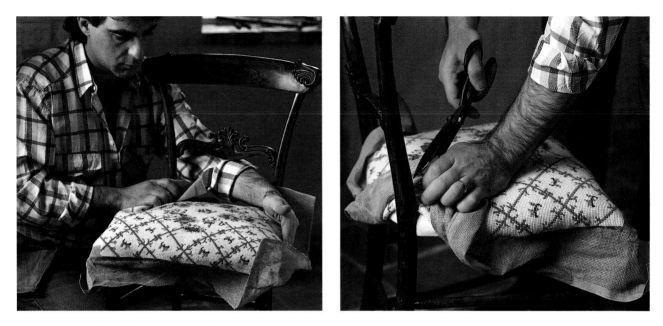

*The finished Tailor of Gloucester canvas being fitted as a seat cover*

## CHART 9

| 384 | | 3197 | | 503 | | 432 | | 402 | |
| 69 | | 712 | | 215 | | 700 | | 635 | |
| 67 | | 736 | | 188 | | 3230 | | | |

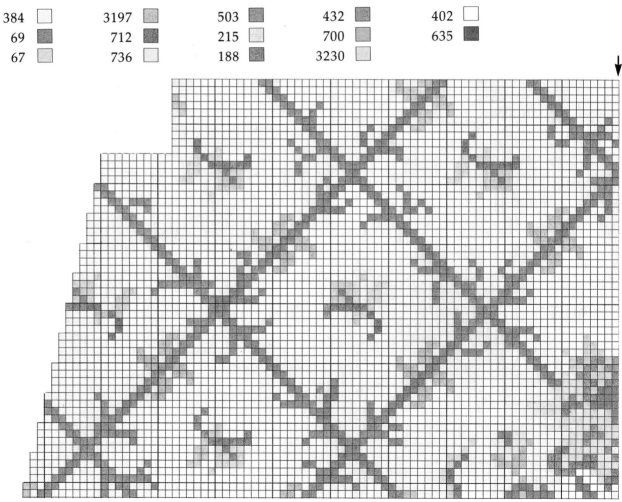

# TAILOR OF GLOUCESTER TAPESTRY WORK BAG

*The Tailor of Gloucester trellis and floral background pattern is extremely versatile, as this work bag*

*shows. The charming design lends itself to a variety of uses: from cushions to a writing-case cover.*

**MEASUREMENTS**

Finished work bag size: approximately 40 cm wide by 42 cm deep/15¾ in wide by 16¾ in deep for each side.

**MATERIALS**

**Anchor Tapisserie Wool**

24 skeins of colour 384, 7 skeins of colour 69, 2 skeins of colour 3197, 1 skein each of colours 67, 215 and 712.

2 pieces of 10-mesh double thread canvas 56 cm wide and 58 cm long/22 in wide and 23 in long. A size 18 tapestry needle. Suitable lining fabric 91 by 46 cm/36 by 18 in. Matching sewing thread. Two bag handles with approximately 25–30 cm/10–12 in slots.

**TO MAKE**

Work in trammed gros point. For preparing your canvas and blocking it, see pages 10 and 11.

Mark the approximate outline of the appropriate section of chart 9 to be worked on each piece of canvas, 156 crossed threads wide by 148 crossed threads high. Commence at top left-hand corner for this tapestry.

The marked 37-stitch square on the chart is repeated 4 times widthwise and lengthwise. Work the remaining 8 stitches to fill in right-hand edge.

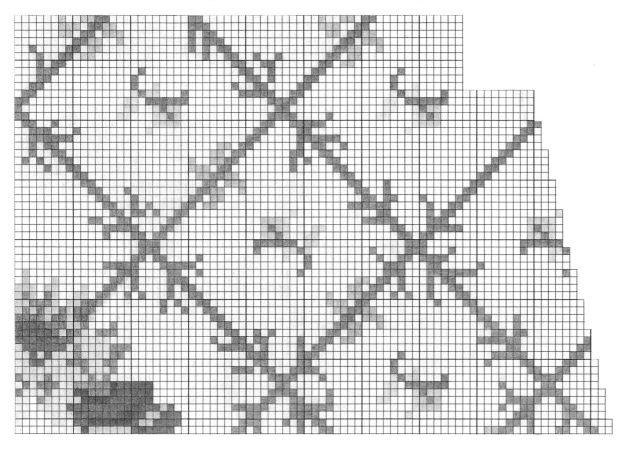

With the right sides of both needlepoints together, backstitch lower edges and a further 20 cm/8 in of each lower side edge. Trim side and lower edges of canvas to within about 5 holes of needlepoint. Lightly hem trimmed turnings of each upper side section to wrong side of needlepoint. Turn out to right side.

Cut 2 pieces of lining the same size as needlepoint pieces plus approximately 1 cm/½ in turning at side and lower edges. Join the lower edges of the lining and a further 20 cm/8 in of the lower side edges. Press open, including unstitched section.

Slip top edges of needlepoint through handle slots and hem neatly in position, pushing up excess fabric as you go to facilitate sewing. Insert lining and hem in position all round.

*Below: Tailor of Gloucester tapestry work bag*                *Above: Detail of tapestry pattern for chair seat and bag*

# LACY STOLE

_The Tailor of Gloucester, set in 'the time of swords and periwigs and full-skirted coats with flowered lappets', inspired me to create this beautiful lacy evening stole; the photograph on page 50 shows how well it complements the tapestry stool cover and work bag._

## MEASUREMENTS

Finished stole size: approximately 43 cm wide and 162 cm long/17 in wide and 64 in long, excluding fringes, after pressing.

## MATERIALS

**Patons Cotton Perle** (50 g balls)
9 balls
A pair of 5½ mm/No 5 needles.

## TENSION

Instructions are based on a standard stocking-stitch tension of 22 sts and 30 rows to 10 cm/4 in on 4 mm needles.

## ABBREVIATIONS

K = knit; p = purl; sts = stitches; rep = repeat; tw3 = insert needle purlwise into next 3 sts as if to p together but instead (p1, k1, p1) into these 3 sts together as though they were one.

## TO MAKE

Cast on 97 sts.
**1st row:** K5, (tw3, k1) to last 4 sts, k4.
**2nd row:** K4, p to last 4 sts, k4.
**3rd to 8th rows:** Rep 1st and 2nd rows 3 times.
**9th row:** K.
**10th row:** K4, p to last 4 sts, k4.
**11th to 16th rows:** Rep 9th and 10th rows 3 times.
Rep these 16 rows until work measures approximately 162 cm/64 in, ending after a 7th row. Cast off.

Press on wrong side following pressing instructions on yarn band. Cut remaining yarn into 25 cm/10 in lengths and, taking 6 strands together for every knot, fringe the short ends. Press and trim tassels.

_The illustration below of the little lady mouse from_ The Tailor of Gloucester _shows how Beatrix Potter enjoyed painting elaborate costume and embroidered fabric_

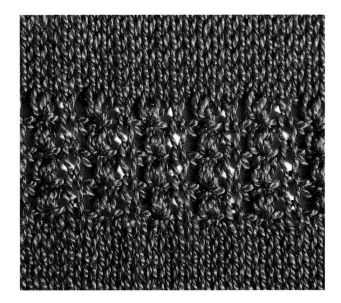

# TAILOR OF GLOUCESTER MOUSE PICTURE

*Here is one of the busy mice from* The Tailor of Gloucester, *just about to thread his needle. It makes a delightful picture for a child's room, or you could hang it by the chair you usually sit in for sewing, as inspiration! What a good present for a needlepointing friend, too.*

**MEASUREMENTS**

Finished tapestry size: approximately 22 cm/8¾ in square.

**MATERIALS**

**Anchor Tapisserie Wool**

3 skeins of colour 384, 2 skeins of colour 712, then 1 skein each of colours 188, 69, 215, 436, 984, 401, 402, 67, 498 and 162.

10-mesh double thread canvas 38 cm/15 in square. A size 18 tapestry needle. A picture frame with backing board to fit.

**TO MAKE**

Follow chart 10, working the entire canvas in half cross stitch. Follow the instructions on pages 10 and 11 for preparing your canvas and blocking it. Mark the centre of the canvas widthwise and lengthwise with a line of basting stitches. Commence the work at the centre and work outwards from this point. When chart is complete, work an additional 4 rows in 712 all round.

Mount your canvas on the backing board, following the instructions and diagrams on pages 10 and 11.

*Two illustrations from* The Tailor of Gloucester

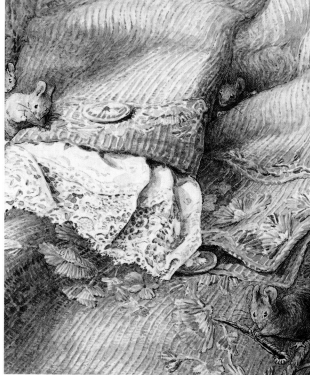

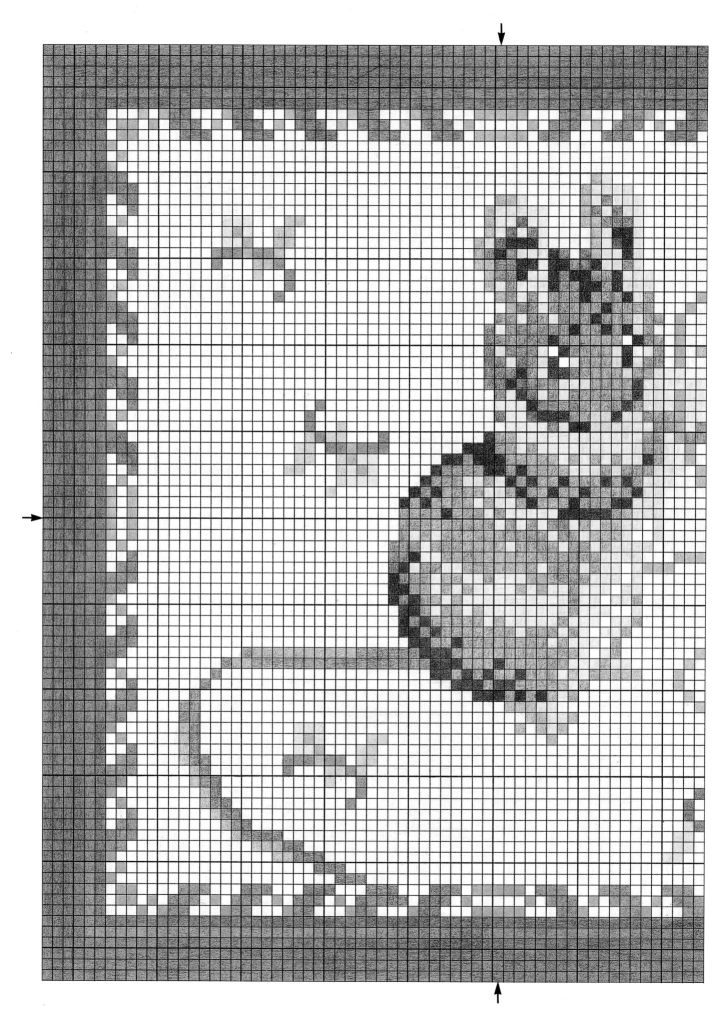

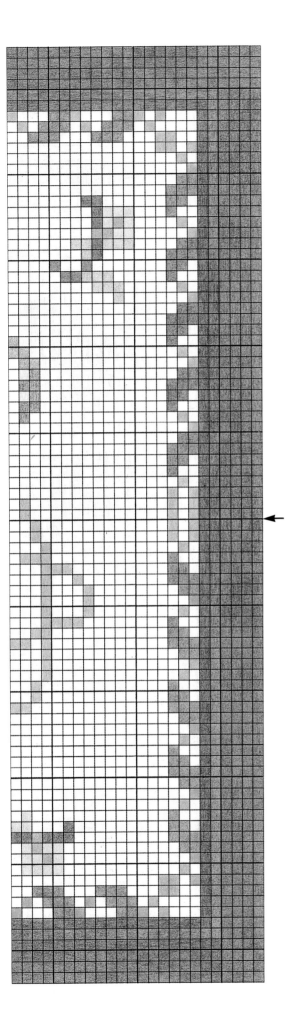

## CHART 10

| | | | | |
|---|---|---|---|---|
| 384 | ☐ | 984 | ▨ |
| 712 | ▨ | 401 | ■ |
| 188 | ▨ | 402 | ☐ |
| 69 | ▨ | 67 | ☐ |
| 215 | ☐ | 498 | ▨ |
| 436 | ☐ | 162 | ▨ |

'There was a snippeting of scissors, and snappeting of thread.'
*From* The Tailor of Gloucester

## LAKELAND LANDSCAPE PICTURE

### 'March Clouds Over Ennerdale'

_____

*This picture was created from a superb photograph
I chose from a collection taken by my uncle some
twenty years ago. I have only departed from the
original print by adding the sheep and a dry-stone
wall, to give some foreground interest.
My uncle has been doing needlepoint for many years
(the photograph shows him at work), and offered
to work the tapestry for me. A complicated design, it
has the effect of an oil painting which is very pleasing
in a softly lit room.*

## MEASUREMENTS

Finished tapestry size, excluding border: approximately 48 cm wide by 36 cm high/19 in wide by 14½ in high.

## MATERIALS

### Anchor Tapisserie Wool

8 skeins of colour 729, 4 skeins each of colours 3094, 144, 402 and 401, 3 skeins of colour 440, 2 skeins each of colours 707, 403, 736, 636, 3087, 861, 984 and 398, and 1 skein each of colours 623, 653, 95, 399, 3013, 732, 397, 3057, 123 and 3124.

### Coats Anchor Stranded Cotton

1 skein of colour 1.
12-mesh double thread canvas 61 cm wide and 51 cm high/24 in wide and 20 in high. A size 22 tapestry needle. Frame and backing board to fit.

## TO MAKE

Work in half cross stitch throughout, using tapisserie wool or 12 strands of stranded cotton. Follow the instructions on pages 10 and 11 for preparing your canvas and blocking it.

Following chart 11, mark the centre of the canvas widthwise and lengthwise with a line of basting stitches. Commence work at centre and work outwards from this point.

Finally, work 2 rows all round in 401, then 14 rows in 729. Finish with a further 2 rows in 729 along lower edge and 2 side edges.

Mount your canvas on the backing board, following the instructions and diagrams on pages 10 and 11.

**CHART 11**

| | | | |
|---|---|---|---|
| 707 | ■ | 636 | ▨ |
| 403 | ■ | 401 | ■ |
| 3094 | ▨ | 3124 | ▨ |
| 144 | ▨ | 402 | ☐ |
| 736 | ▨ | 3087 | ▨ |

64

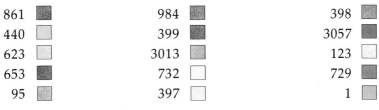

| 861 | | 984 | | 398 | |
| 440 | | 399 | | 3057 | |
| 623 | | 3013 | | 123 | |
| 653 | | 732 | | 729 | |
| 95 | | 397 | | 1 | |

# HILL TOP BY NIGHT PICTURE

*A tapestry recreation of one of my favourite Beatrix Potter watercolours. I love the warmth of the farmhouse lights flooding out on to the snow and the bold, almost modern, feel of the painting. The picture is easy and quick to make, as it is worked in long stitch.*

**MEASUREMENTS**

Finished tapestry size: approximately 18½ cm wide by 25 cm high/7½ in wide by 10 in high.

**MATERIALS**

**Anchor Tapisserie Wool**

4 skeins of colour 3034, 2 skeins of colour 3197, then 1 skein each of colours 3195, 3199, 506, 837, 402, 738 and 625.

**Coats Anchor Stranded Cotton**

1 skein each of colours 1, 301 and 303.

16-mesh lockweave canvas 33 cm wide by 41 cm high/13 in wide by 16 in high. A size 18 tapestry needle. Frame and backing board to fit.

*Below: A wintry scene painted in about 1910*

**TO MAKE**

Follow chart 12, using tapisserie wool or 9 strands of stranded cotton.

Work in vertical long stitch throughout. Follow the instructions on pages 10 and 11 for preparing your canvas and blocking it.

The tree branches in the top left-hand corner, indicated by broken lines, are worked last in stem stitch in 625 and superimposed on the long stitch.

To work the border, work 2 rows of satin stitch over 8 threads in 3034 on all sides, mitring the corners (see photograph below). The satin stitch on the side edges is worked horizontally.

Mount your canvas on the backing board, following the instructions and diagrams on pages 10 and 11.

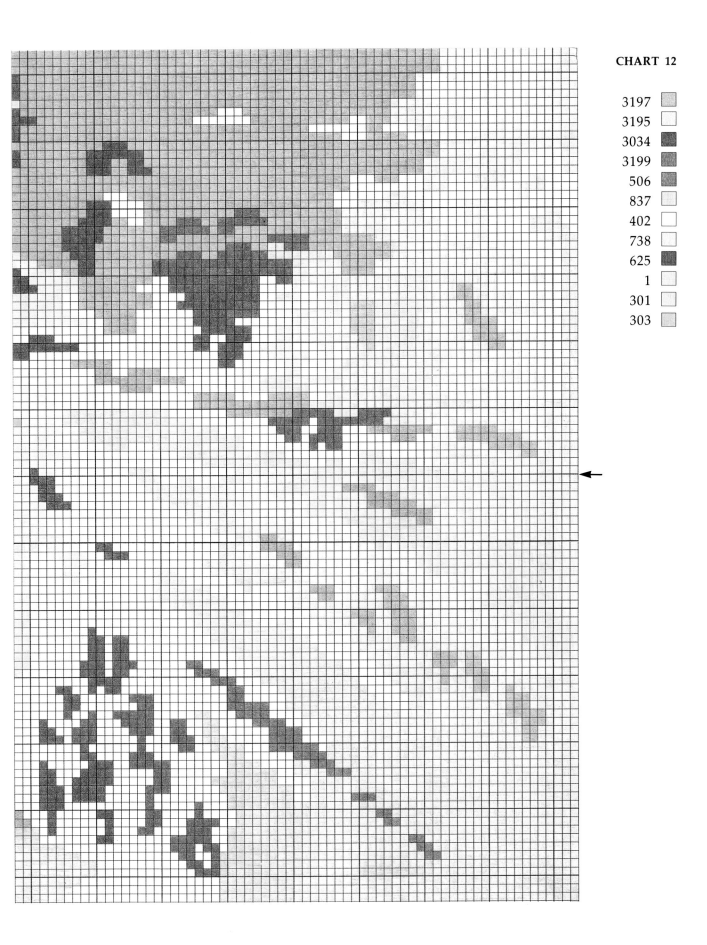

CHART 12

3197
3195
3034
3199
506
837
402
738
625
1
301
303

# CRADLE OR PRAM COVER

## Knitted, with over-embroidery

*The picture of Mrs. Tittlemouse asleep in her little box bed, complete with cosy coverlet, was the inspiration for this lovely knitted cover. The pastel colours are suitable for either boys or girls, and the zig-zag design, embroidered eyelets and thick tassels make the blanket really special.*

**MEASUREMENTS**
Finished cover size: 76 × 86 cm/30 × 34 in.

**MATERIALS**
**Patons Fairytale DK** (100 g balls)
2 balls in White (M) and 1 ball each in Pink (A), Blue (B) and Lemon (C).
A pair of 4½ mm/No 7 needles.

**TENSION**
Instructions are based on a standard stocking-stitch tension of 22 sts and 30 rows to 10 cm/4 in on 4½ mm needles.

**ABBREVIATIONS**
K = knit; p = purl; sts = stitches; patt = pattern; tog = together; yfwd = yarn forward; sl = slip; psso = pass slipped stitch over.

**TO MAKE**
With M, cast on 175 sts loosely. Joining in and breaking off colours as required, work in patt thus:
**1st to 4th rows:** In M, k.
**5th row:** In A, k3, k2tog, (k10, yfwd, k1, yfwd, k10, sl 1, k2tog, psso) 6 times, k10, yfwd, k1, yfwd, k10, sl 1, k1, psso, k3.
**6th row:** In A, k3, p to last 3 sts, k3.
**7th and 8th rows:** As 5th and 6th.
**9th row:** In A, k3, k2tog, (k3, k2tog, yfwd, k5, yfwd, k1, yfwd, k5, yfwd, sl 1, k1, psso, k3, sl 1, k2tog, psso) 6 times, k3, k2tog, yfwd, k5, yfwd, k1, yfwd, k5, yfwd, sl 1, k1, psso, k3, sl 1, k1, psso, k3.
**10th row:** As 6th.

**11th to 14th rows:** Repeat 5th and 6th rows twice.
**15th to 28th rows:** As 1st to 14th rows but working rows 5 to 14 in B.
**29th to 42nd rows:** As 1st to 14th rows but working rows 5 to 14 in C.
Repeat the last 42 rows 3 times *more*, then rows 1 to 14 again.
**Next 5 rows:** K in M (on next row fabric will be reversed for top to fold back).
Commencing with 19th row, work 42 more rows in patt.
Knit 1 more row in M.
Cast off loosely in M.

Embroider each single eyelet, working a 5-petal lazy daisy in M around each hole. Make 8 tassels in M or desired colour and attach to points at lower edge. Press following pressing instructions on ball band.

*Below: From* The Tale of Mrs. Tittlemouse

# MRS. TITTLEMOUSE BASKET LID

*Dear Mrs. Tittlemouse, she does look so tired! I can remember this picture from when I was very small. Now, it reflects how I often feel after a hard day! I was very pleased with myself for managing to make her eyes look closed – features are not easy when there are so few stitches to manipulate. As well as a basket lid, the tapestry can also be used to make a circular padded picture or stool top.*

## MEASUREMENTS
Finished lid size: approximately 25 cm/10 in across.

## MATERIALS
**Paterna Tapestry Wool** (8 yd skeins)
6 skeins of colour 534, 5 skeins of colour 444, 2 skeins each of colours 434, 462, 464, D143 and 948, and 1 skein each of colours 804, 460, 443, 475, 261, 946 and 934.
10-mesh interlock canvas 46 cm/18 in square. A size 18 tapestry needle. A circular basket with lid to fit. Padding. Braid and studs for edging.

## TO MAKE
Follow chart 13 overleaf, using 3 strands of wool.

Work the entire canvas in continental tent stitch. Follow the instructions on pages 10 and 11 for preparing your canvas and blocking it.
Mark the centre of the canvas widthwise and lengthwise with a line of basting stitches. Commence work at the centre and continue to work outwards from this point.

Pad the top of the lid with wadding. Lay the canvas centrally over the wadding and, using fine tacks, pull into shape and secure evenly all round.
Excess canvas may be cut away or tucked up inside. Finish the basket lid or picture by edging it with braid and studs.

*'She was too tired to do any more.' From* The Tale of Mrs. Tittlemouse

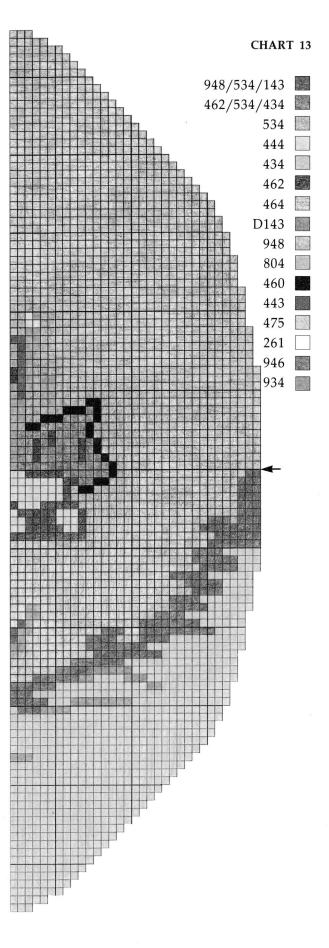

**CHART 13**

| | |
|---|---|
| 948/534/143 | ■ |
| 462/534/434 | ■ |
| 534 | □ |
| 444 | □ |
| 434 | □ |
| 462 | ■ |
| 464 | ▦ |
| D143 | ▦ |
| 948 | ▦ |
| 804 | □ |
| 460 | ■ |
| 443 | ■ |
| 475 | ▦ |
| 261 | □ |
| 946 | ▦ |
| 934 | ▦ |

# PETER RABBIT RUG

### Circular tufted rug

_____

*Coming at the beginning of the first Beatrix Potter book I ever owned, this must be the picture I recall best from my childhood days. A sketch by Beatrix Potter still exists showing the actual fir tree 'near Keswick' which she used as the basis for the illustration, and the realism of this animal family scene is unfailingly appealing. I couldn't resist including it somewhere.*

## MEASUREMENTS
Finished rug size: 91 cm/36 in across.

## MATERIALS
**Nottingham Group Turkey Action packs** (160 pieces per pack)
13 of colour 973, 10 each of colours 928 and 930, 9 of colour 939, 7 of colour 900, 6 of colour 940, 4 each of colours 983, 901 and 975, 3 each of colours 501, 932 and 858, 2 each of colours 888, 961, 957 and 978, and 1 each of colours 941, 52 and 50.
**Nottingham Group Rug Wool** (50 g balls)
3 balls in colour 973.
3⅓-mesh interlock rug canvas 91 cm wide and 102 cm long/36 in wide and 40 in long. Latchet hook. Carpet braid. Matching sewing thread.

## TO MAKE
See the instructions for rug-making given on pages 29 and 15. Work from chart 35 overleaf, starting the row of knots across the starting edge of the design. Bind the edge of the rug with colour 973 rug wool, as shown on page 17.

## RUG CARE AND CLEANING
See page 29, Oak Leaves and Ribbon rug.

CHART 35

| 973 | | 900 | | 975 | | 888 | | 941 | |
| 928 | | 940 | | 501 | | 961 | | 52 | |
| 930 | | 983 | | 932 | | 957 | | 50 | |
| 939 | | 901 | | 858 | | 978 | | | |

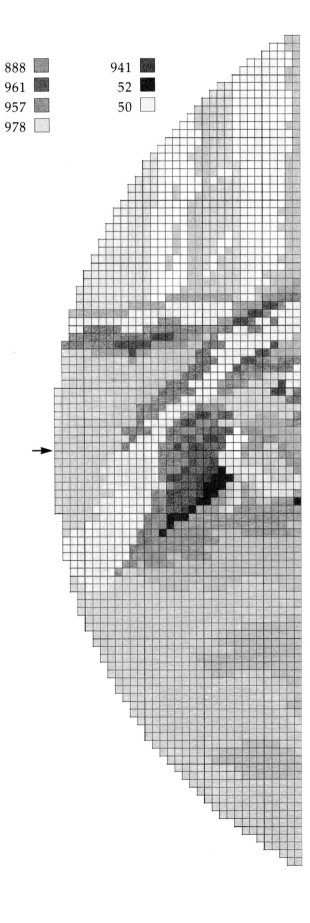

*'Once upon a time there were four little Rabbits . . .' From* The Tale of Peter Rabbit

# FUNGI AND ROSEHIPS BASKET LID

---

*Beatrix Potter was a great fungi enthusiast, and painted many species in meticulous detail. I wanted to include one of these studies in the book, and particularly liked a watercolour of a group of brown Amanita aspera. Embellished with some rosehips from another painting, the round shapes and composition of the group make a very pleasing circular basket lid. The canvas could also be used as a stool cover or padded picture.*

**MEASUREMENTS**
Finished lid size: approximately 36 cm/14 in across.

**MATERIALS**
**Paterna Tapestry Wool** (8 yd skeins)
22 skeins of colour 615, 9 skeins of colour 643,
5 skeins of colour 756, 3 skeins each of colours 436
and 413, 2 skeins each of colours 401, 472, 410, 260
and 256, and 1 skein each of colours 744, 419, 881,
862, 516, 603 and 850.

10-mesh interlock canvas 51 cm/20 in square. A
size 18 tapestry needle. A circular basket with lid to
fit. Padding. Braid and studs for edging.

**TO MAKE**
Following chart 14, work as given for the Mrs.
Tittlemouse basket lid on page 73.

*Below: Beatrix Potter's painting of* Amanita aspera. *She studied fungi while on holiday in Scotland and the Lake District.*

CHART 14

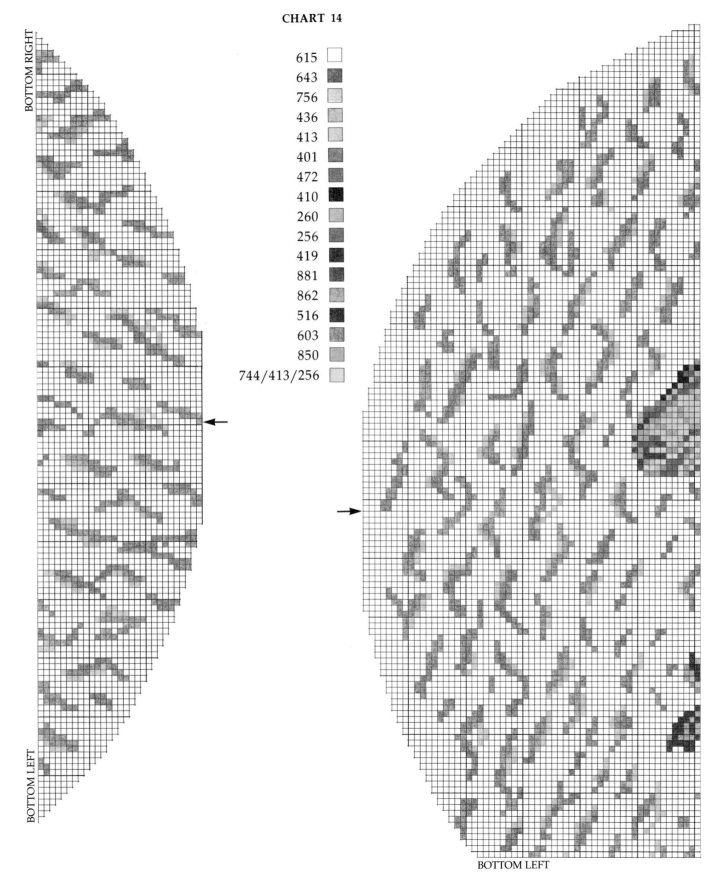

| | |
|---|---|
| 615 | |
| 643 | |
| 756 | |
| 436 | |
| 413 | |
| 401 | |
| 472 | |
| 410 | |
| 260 | |
| 256 | |
| 419 | |
| 881 | |
| 862 | |
| 516 | |
| 603 | |
| 850 | |
| 744/413/256 | |

BOTTOM RIGHT

BOTTOM LEFT

BOTTOM LEFT

80

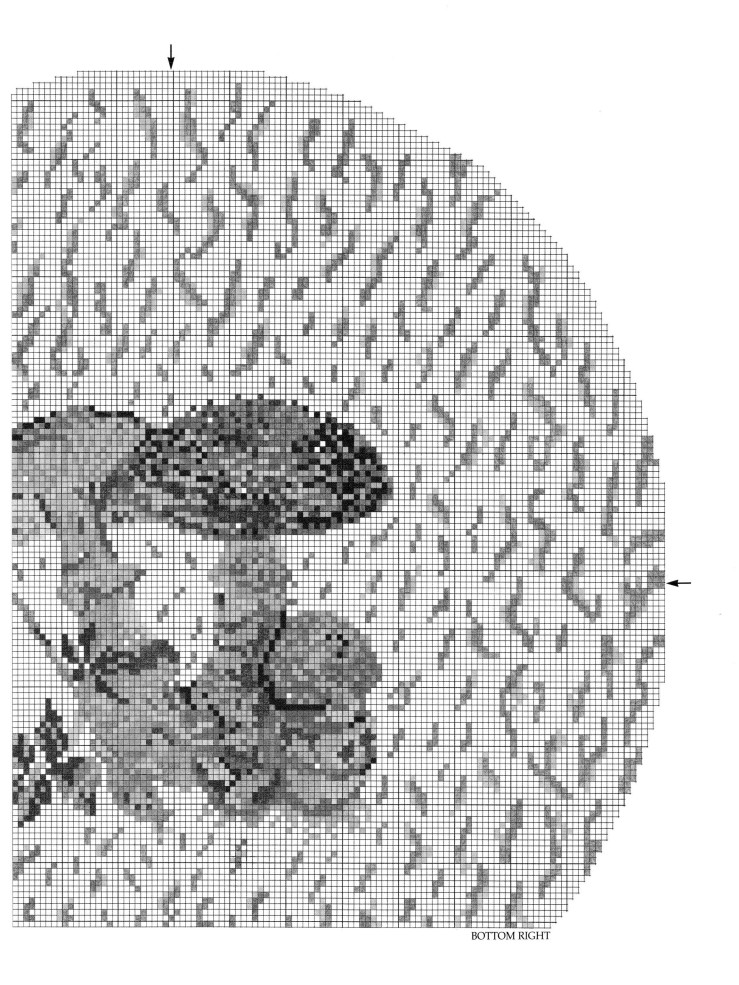

BOTTOM RIGHT

# COTTAGE AFGHAN

*Beatrix Potter left many sketches of rugs and warmers of various sorts, and her picture book characters are often adorned in shawls and plaids. I have tried to capture here a patchwork, textured effect, worked in colours to reflect the cushion. The afghan looks wonderful against dark oak, and is lovely to snuggle round you on a cold winter's evening.*

## MEASUREMENTS
Finished rug size: approximately 114 × 122 cm/ 45 × 48 in.

## MATERIALS
**Patons Beehive Shetland Chunky** (50 g balls) 18 balls in Cream (M) and 2 balls each in Dark Blue (A), Brown (B), Yellow (C) and Light Blue (D). A pair of 6½ mm/No 3 needles. A cable needle.

## TENSION
Instructions are based on a tension of 17 sts and 24 rows to 10 cm/4 in over the 2-tone pattern area.

## ABBREVIATIONS
K = knit; p = purl; sts = stitches; patt = pattern; rep = repeat; slp = slip next st purlways; C7 = slip next 3 sts on cable needle to front of work (i.e. towards you), p1, k2, p1, now k2, p1 from cable needle; tog = together.

## TO MAKE
FIRST STRIP (make 6)
With M, cast on 23 sts. Work in patt thus:
**1st and 2nd rows:** In M, k.
**3rd row:** In A, k3, (slp with yarn back, k3) to end.
**4th row:** In A, k1, p2, (slp with yarn front – i.e. towards you – p3) to last 4 sts, slp, p2, k1.
**5th to 12th rows:** Rep 1st to 4th rows twice.

*The Cottage afghan, Sad Rabbit cushion and floral stool displayed with Beatrix Potter's rocking chair and hanging utensils in the kitchen at Hill Top*

**13th row:** In M, (k2, k2tog) to last 3 sts, k2tog, k1 (*17 sts*). Continue in M only.
**14th row:** K.
**15th row:** K1, p1, (k1, p2) to last 3 sts, k1, p1, k1.
**16th row:** K2, (p1, k2) to end.
**17th to 21st rows:** Rep 15th and 16th rows twice, then 15th row again.
**22nd row:** K2, p1, k2, C7, k2, p1, k2.
**23rd to 27th rows:** Rep 15th and 16th rows twice, then 15th row again.
**28th row:** (k2, make 1 by picking up and knitting into back of horizontal thread lying before next st, p1) to last 2 sts, make 1, k2. (*23 sts*)
**29th to 56th rows:** Rep 1st to 28th rows *but* using B in place of A.
Rep these 56 rows 3 times more, then first 40 rows again.
Cast off. Make 5 *more* strips the same.

SECOND STRIP (make 5)
With M, cast on 17 sts.
Work rows 15 to 28 as 1st strip.
Now work rows 1 to 14 but using C in place of A.
Work rows 15 to 28 again.
Finally, work rows 1 to 14 again but using D in place of A.
Rep these 56 rows 3 times more, then first 40 rows again.
Cast off. Work 4 *more* strips the same.

## TO MAKE UP
Press following instructions on ball band. Using a flat seam, join strips neatly, alternating as you go.

# THE SAD RABBIT CUSHION

CHART 16

## MEASUREMENTS

Finished cushion size: approximately 41 cm/16 in square.

## MATERIALS

**Paterna Persian Yarn** (8 yd skeins)

16 skeins of colour 502, 13 skeins of colour 505, 3 skeins of colour 260, 2 skeins each of colours 262 and 475, then 1 skein each of colours 463, 436, 451, 402, 443, 256, 420, 772, 710 and 605.

10-mesh single thread canvas 56 cm/22 in square.

A size 18 tapestry needle. A piece of backing fabric 43 cm/17 in square. A cushion pad to fit. Matching sewing thread. Braid.

## TO MAKE

Follow chart 16. First mark the centre of the canvas widthwise and lengthwise with a line of basting stitches.

Commence at the centre and work in continental tent stitch throughout, following the instructions on pages 10 and 11 for preparing your canvas and blocking it.

Complete as for the squirrel cushion on page 26.

*From an illustration from* The Story of A Fierce Bad Rabbit

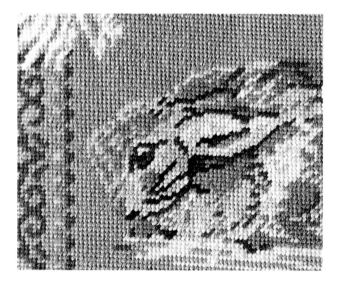

502
505
260
262
475
463
436
451
402
443
256
420
772
710
605

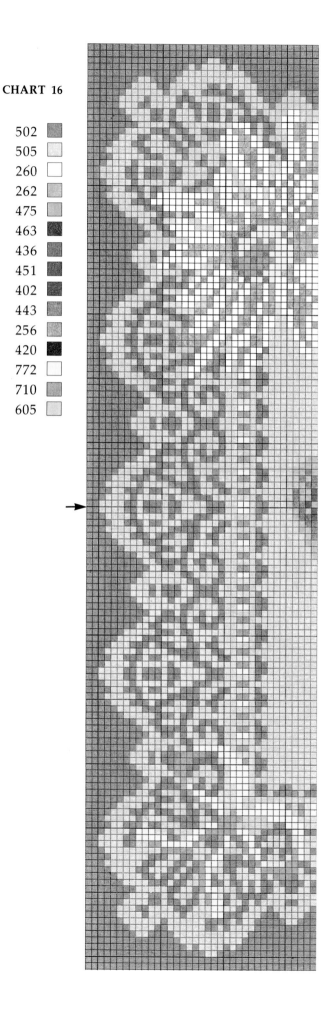

## BIRTH SAMPLER

### Counted cross stitch

---

*This sampler is a pot-pourri of Potter designs, with some additions of my own in keeping with the Victorian feel. The daisies come from a watercolour by Beatrix Potter, Babbitty Bumble from* The Tale of Mrs. Tittlemouse *hovers by a foxglove, and Hunca Munca proudly rocks her babies in their cradle stolen from the doll's house in* The Tale of Two Bad Mice. *The initials at the top of the sampler are those of Rupert Potter and Helen Leech, Beatrix's parents, and her full name has been worked. The choice of frame for your sampler is very important. I found an old frame and had it cut up to fit the piece.*

*From* The Tale of Two Bad Mice

## MEASUREMENTS
Approximate size of sampler when framed: 29 × 26 cm/11¾ × 10¼ in.

## MATERIALS
The following quantities are the correct amounts for the 5 charts only and do not allow for any additional freehand motifs you may wish to add.
**Coats Anchor Stranded Cotton**
1 skein each of colours 1, 933, 375, 386, 1201, 1216, 832, 831, 905, 403, 49, 23, 43, 976, 779 and 291.
19-mesh Pure Linen Cork approximately 33 × 38 cm/13 × 15 in. A size 24 or 26 tapestry needle. A picture frame with backing board to fit.

N.B. If you wish to work the sampler on a larger or finer mesh fabric this will be quite possible, but of course the quantities required may need adjusting accordingly, also the number of strands used.

## TO MAKE
Follow the instructions on pages 10 and 11 for preparing your canvas.
First place a vertical tack through centre of fabric, then place a horizontal tack about 2 cm/1 in above centre of fabric.
Using 2 strands of cotton, working in cross stitch throughout, work chart 17 ensuring that top stitches of crosses all lie in same direction, first lining up arrows 1, 2, 3 and 4 to correspond with the cross-way tacks.
Leaving 19 sts free *above* chart 17, outline chart 18 with a tack, 95 sts wide and 38 sts deep, lining up arrow 3 with centre vertical tack.
Now work chart 18.
Leaving 22 sts free *below* chart 17, outline chart 21 with a tack 161 sts wide and 57 sts deep, lining up arrow 4 with centre vertical tack.
Now work chart 21.
Leaving 13 sts free to *left* of chart 17, lining up arrow 1 with centre horizontal tack, outline chart 19, 35 sts wide by 124 sts deep.
Now work chart 19.

Finally, leaving 13 sts free to *right* of chart 17, outline chart 20 and work.

Press work carefully on wrong side using a warm iron and a damp cloth. Mount your embroidery on the backing board, following the instructions and diagrams on pages 10 and 11.

*This running rabbit is the best known of all Beatrix Potter's images. It originally also appeared inside the book but was taken out later to make room for pictorial endpapers.*

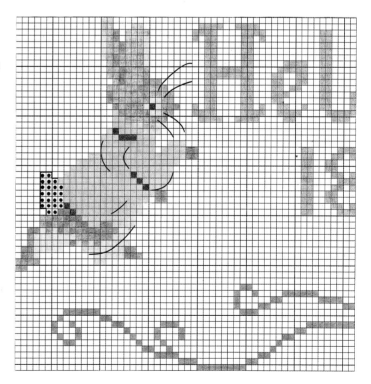

88

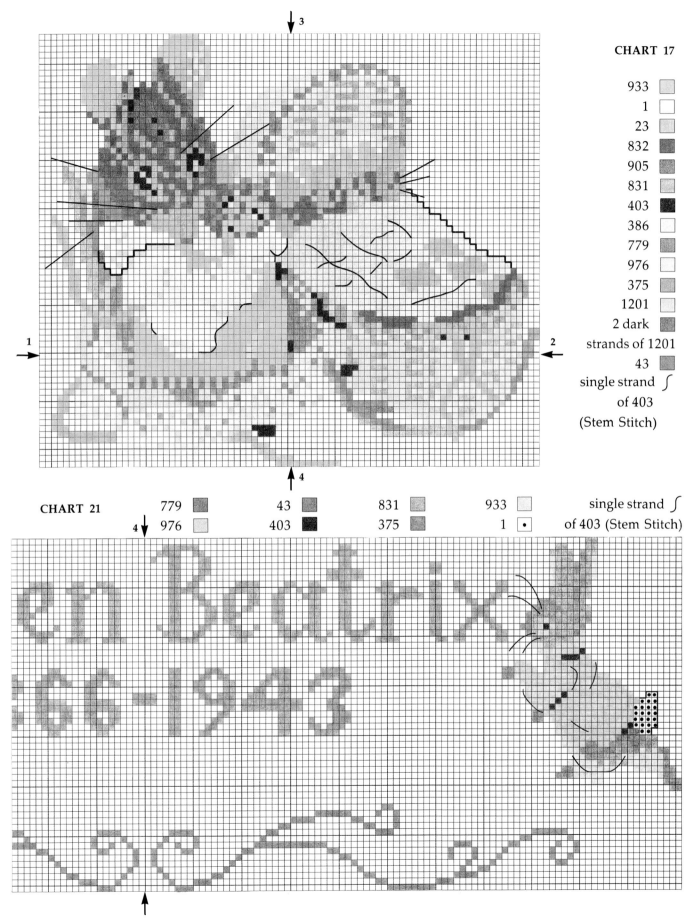

**CHART 17**

933
1
23
832
905
831
403
386
779
976
375
1201
2 dark
strands of 1201
43
single strand ∫
of 403
(Stem Stitch)

**CHART 21**

779    43    831    933    single strand ∫
976    403    375    1    •    of 403 (Stem Stitch)

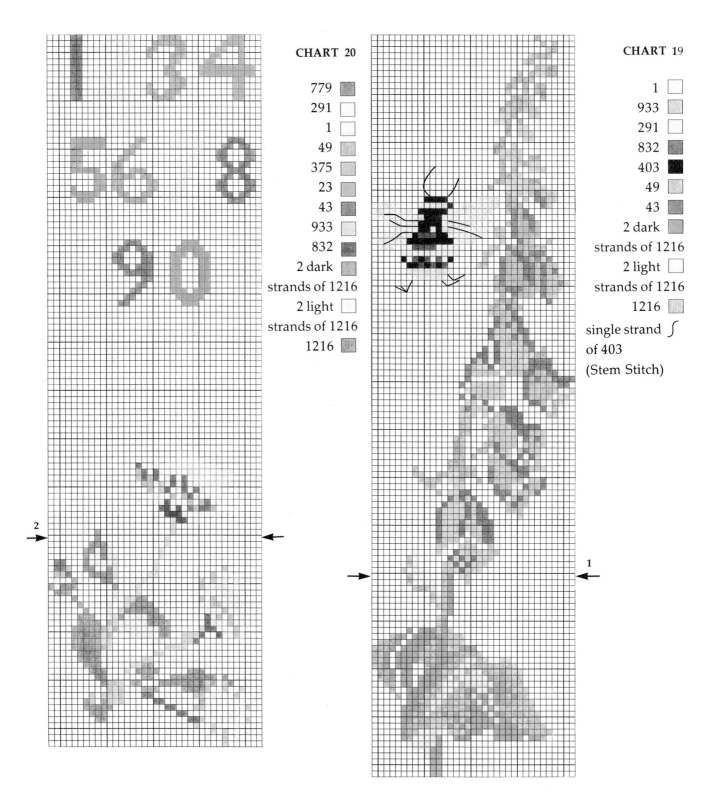

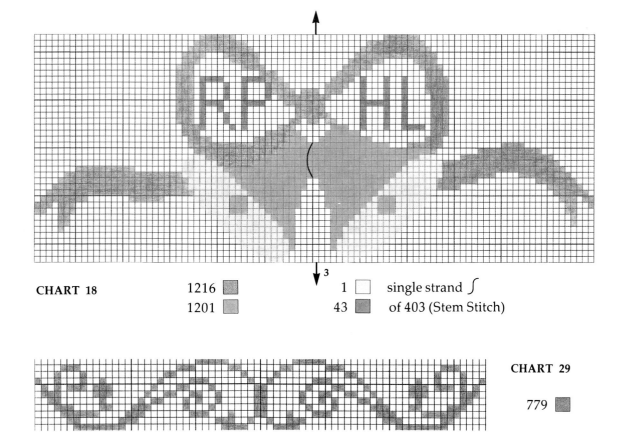

**CHART 18**

1216 ▨
1201 ▨

1 ☐
43 ▨

single strand ∫
of 403 (Stem Stitch)

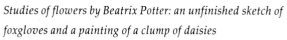

**CHART 29**

779 ▨

*Studies of flowers by Beatrix Potter: an unfinished sketch of foxgloves and a painting of a clump of daisies*

# FOXGLOVE BELL PULL

*The birth sampler on page 86 contains several details which may be used on their own in all sorts of ways. This novel wall-hanging features the foxglove from the sampler (as seen in* The Tale of Jemima Puddle-Duck *and many other of Beatrix Potter's paintings), with Babbitty Bumble from* The Tale of Mrs. Tittlemouse *hovering nearby. A decorative border completes the design.*

**MEASUREMENTS**
Finished size of embroidery only: 25 cm long by 10 cm wide/10 in long by 4 in wide.

**MATERIALS**
**Coats Anchor Stranded Cotton**
1 skein each of colours 933, 49, 43, 1, 1216, 403, 291, 832 and 779.
14-mesh Ecru Aida embroidery material 20 cm wide and 36 cm long/8 in wide and 14 in long. A size 18 tapestry needle. Iron-on interlining and backing fabric to fit. Tassel and cord. 2 short lengths of picture frame.

**TO MAKE**
Overcast the raw edges to avoid fraying, as recommended on pages 10 and 11. Follow chart 19, using 2 strands of cotton throughout. Each square represents one intersection on the Aida. Work the entire embroidery in cross stitch, making sure all top stitches run in the same direction.
First mark the centre of fabric widthwise and lengthwise with a line of basting stitches. Ignoring arrows and 'Fig. 1', which refer to another design, mark a pencil arrow at each vertical side edge between the 62nd and 63rd stitches on chart 19. Similarly, mark the centre of the upper and lower edges of chart 19.
Start from the centre of the design and count outwards. Finish each length by running it under a few stitches.
When chart 19 is complete, continue stalk of foxglove down a further 16 rows. If desired, outline

the flower bells with a single strand of colour 43 in backstitch. Remove tacks.
Now, leaving 4 blocks of threads free at left side edge, work chart 29 in cross stitch, placing top row of chart level with top of foxglove. Repeat chart 29 underneath first section worked. Turn chart round and repeat border on right-hand edge to correspond.

Press the embroidery on the wrong side under a damp cloth. Cut the interlining to correspond with the desired finished size of embroidery, and iron it on to the back of the embroidery.
Place an oddment of fabric over the right side of embroidery. Leaving lower edge open, backstitch round the other 3 sides, close to the edges of interlining. Trim and turn out and sew up the fourth side. Press seams.
Cut frame to fit upper and lower edges and glue or tack embroidery in place. Attach tassel to lower edge and make a cord loop at top edge.

*Below: From* The Tale of Mrs. Tittlemouse

## ROSE RUG

### Stitched rug

_____

*It was the custom for young ladies in Victorian times
to paint flowers, and Beatrix Potter was no exception.
She loved plants and trees, and would study and
paint individual blossoms and leaves many times
over. Later on, she filled her stories with flowers too:
foxgloves, geraniums, tiger lilies, pansies and pinks
all appear, amongst others.*

*The following group of items was based on a
particularly beautiful watercolour of a single rose; the
motif lent itself to a variety of designs and really
inspired my imagination! The medallions on the
bedspread can be used on other things too – from
tray cloths to a tapestry picture.*

*Beatrix Potter's rose, in watercolour and pen-and-ink*

## MEASUREMENTS

Finished rug size: approximately 61 × 88 cm/24 × 34½ in, excluding fringes.

## MATERIALS

**Readicut Rug Wool** (45 g balls)

12 balls of colour G, 5 balls of colour 58, 3 of colour S, 2 of colour H, then 1 ball each of colours 43, Y, C, B, A and D.

**Readicut 2-ply Carpet Wool**

3 hanks of cream wool, for fringes.

5-mesh interlock canvas 69 cm wide by 102 cm long/27 in wide by 40 in long. A size 13 bodkin needle. Latchet hook for fringing. Matching sewing thread.

N.B. If difficulty is experienced in purchasing yarn, see 'Useful Addresses' on pages 126 and 127.

## TO MAKE

It is not essential to work with a frame but, should one be used, a hand-held or floor-standing frame at least 91 cm/36 in wide will make the work easier. If a frame is not used, stretching of the rug into shape when completed may be necessary.

See the note 'Cross stitch for rugs' on page 16, then commence work by placing the canvas on a table or by fixing it to your frame. Begin at the centre and work horizontally as far as possible, filling in blocks of colour and using the chart for reference.

Follow chart 8 and work in cross stitch. Mark the centre of the canvas widthwise and lengthwise with a line of basting stitches; the tacks should correspond with arrows on the chart. Each square represents one intersection on the canvas.

To complete the border, work the upper right-hand quarter in reverse. Then work the left half to match. Fold under excess canvas all round and stitch in position, leaving one row of holes visible at each end for fringing.

**Fringes:** Using a latchet hook, knot two 30 cm/ 12 in lengths into each hole of the two ends, thus forming a row of tassels.

When this has been done, tie the tassels as shown in the diagram on page 16. Trim the fringe evenly and then press, using a warm iron and a damp cloth.

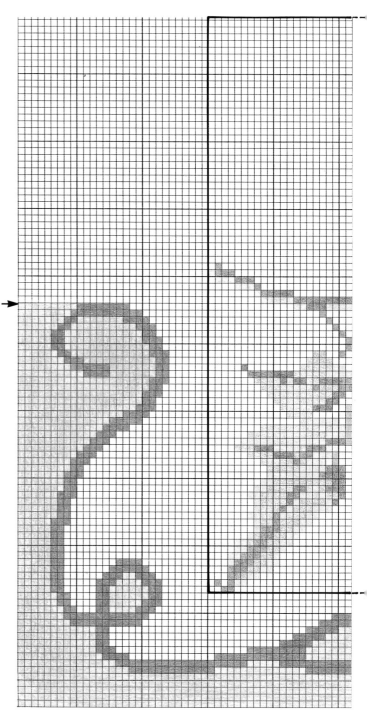

CHART 8
BEDSPREAD AND RUG

G

69, 43

2, Y

68, C

67, S

21, B

15, A

51, 58

6, H

7, D

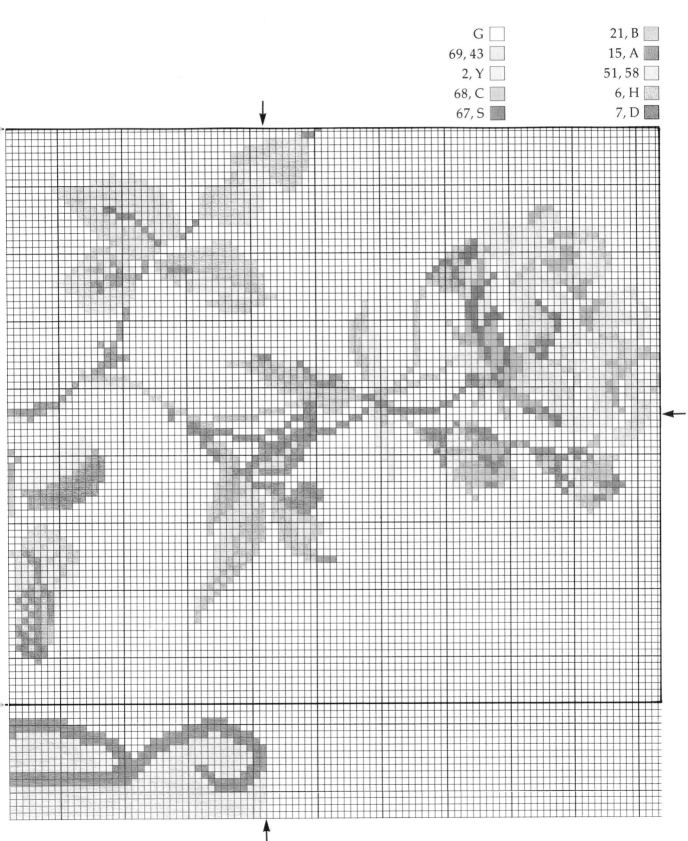

# ROSE TABLECLOTH

## Embroidered, with crochet border

---

**MEASUREMENTS**

Finished tablecloth size, excluding border: 112 cm/ 44 in square.

**MATERIALS**

**Twilley's White Lyscordet** (for border)
6 × 25 g balls.

**Twilley's Lystra Stranded Cotton**
4 skeins of colour 6, 2 each of colours 69, 7, 2, 68 and 21, 1 skein each of colours 67, 15 and 51.
A piece of Salamanca or other suitable embroidery fabric, 114 cm/45 in square. A 2.00 mm crochet hook. Embroidery needle. Matching sewing thread.

**TENSION** (for crochet border)

8 spaces and 8 rows to 5 cm/2 in square.

**ABBREVIATIONS**

Ch = chain; tr = treble; sp = space; rep = repeat.

SPECIAL NOTE: Filet Crochet

While one block – x on charts – is made up of 2 tr worked either into 2 tr or into a tr and a ch sp, a single cross will appear as 3 tr in work; 2 tr for the block and 1 tr belonging to the adjacent sp. Two crosses will appear as 5 tr, 3 crosses as 7 tr and so on.

**TO MAKE BORDER**

Make 31 ch.

**1st row:** 1 tr into 4th ch from hook, 1 tr into next ch, 1 ch, miss 1 ch, 1 tr into next 3 ch, (1 ch, miss next ch, 1 tr into next ch) 10 times, 1 tr into last 2 ch.

**2nd row:** 3 ch (standing as 1st tr), 1 tr into next 2 tr, (1 ch, 1 tr into next tr) 9 times, 1 tr into ch sp, 1 tr into next tr, 1 ch, miss next tr, 1 tr into next tr, 1 tr into ch sp, 1 tr into next tr, turn.

**3rd row:** 4 ch (standing as 1st tr and 1 ch sp), miss next tr, 1 tr into next tr, 1 tr into ch sp, 1 tr into next

tr, 1 ch, miss next tr, 1 tr into next tr, 1 tr into ch sp, 1 tr into next tr, (1 ch, 1 tr into next tr) 8 times, 1 tr into next tr, 1 tr into top of 3 ch.

**4th to 9th rows:** Work rows 4 to 9 from chart.

**10th row:** 3 ch (standing as 1st tr), 1 tr into next 2 tr, (1 ch, 1 tr into next tr) twice, 1 ch, miss next tr, 1 tr into next tr, 1 tr into ch sp, 1 tr into next tr, 1 ch, miss next tr, 1 tr into next tr, 1 tr into ch sp, 1 tr into 3rd of 4 ch.

**11th row:** 8 ch, 1 tr into 7th ch from hook, 1 tr into next ch, 1 tr into next tr, 1 ch, miss next tr, 1 tr into next tr, 1 tr into ch sp, 1 tr into next tr, 1 ch, miss next tr, 1 tr into next tr, (1 ch, 1 tr into next tr) 3 times, 1 tr into next tr, 1 tr into top of 3 ch.

**12th to 16th rows:** Work rows 12 to 16 from chart.

**17th row:** 4 ch, 1 tr into 4th ch from hook, 1 tr into next tr, 1 ch, miss next tr, 1 tr into next tr, 1 tr into ch sp, 1 tr into next tr, 1 ch, miss next tr, 1 tr into next tr, (1 ch, 1 tr into next tr) 9 times, 1 tr into next tr, 1 tr into top of 3 ch.

Now continue from chart, repeating rows 2 to 17 inclusive until border measures approximately 489 cm/193 in, ending after a 16th row. Fasten off.

Pin border out to size and press lightly with a warm iron and a damp cloth. Leave to dry and unpin.

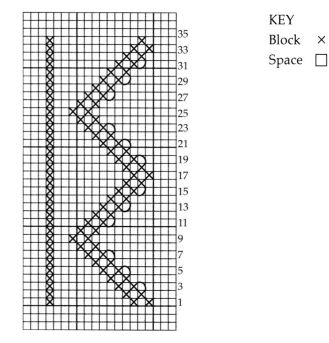

KEY

Block  ×

Space  □

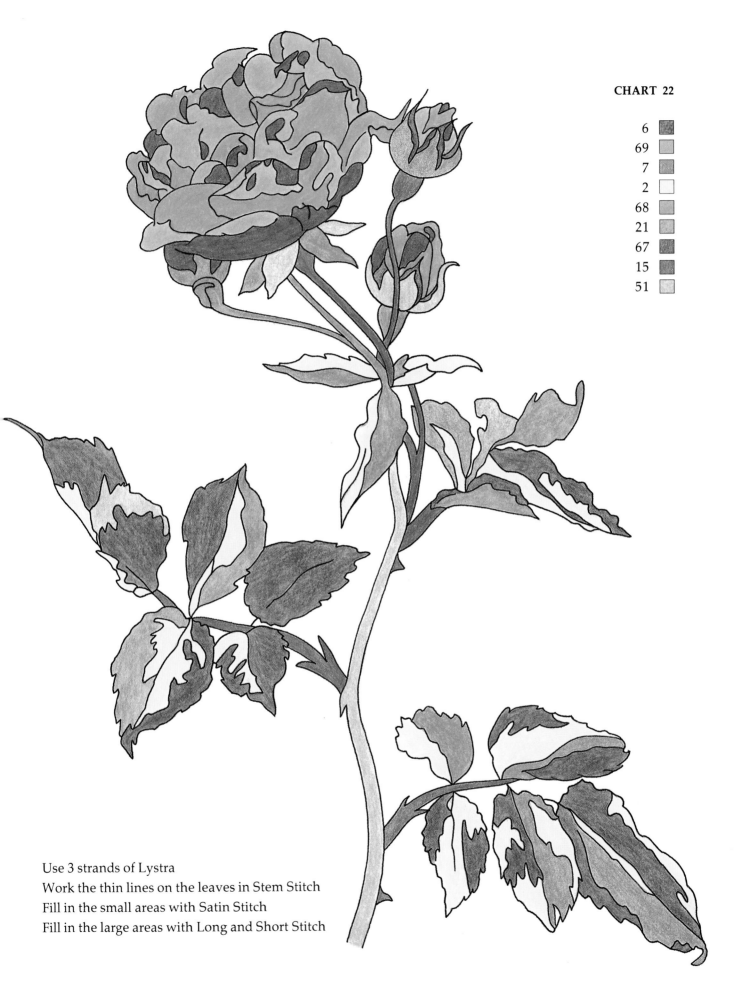

**CHART 22**

6
69
7
2
68
21
67
15
51

Use 3 strands of Lystra
Work the thin lines on the leaves in Stem Stitch
Fill in the small areas with Satin Stitch
Fill in the large areas with Long and Short Stitch

## TO MAKE TABLECLOTH

If necessary, draw a thread on each edge of embroidery fabric to ensure that it is square and trim. Oversew or overlock edges. Trace 4 rose sprays from chart 22 and arrange as desired on the fabric. Transfer image by the old-fashioned pouncing method, or by use of dressmakers' carbon paper or transfer pencil. Follow the directions on the chart as to placing of colours and stitches used. When finished, press lightly on wrong side.

## TO MAKE UP

Join short ends of the border to form a ring. Placing seam at one corner and easing in approximately 1 pattern repeat at each corner, top-stitch border to main part of tablecloth.

*Detail of Rose tablecloth embroidery*

## ROSE BEDSPREAD

Embroidered, with crochet border

---

### MEASUREMENTS

Bedspread fits a standard single bed. Finished top area measures 198 cm long by 91 cm wide/78 in long by 36 in wide; side drop, approximately 56 cm/20 in to lower points.

### MATERIALS

**Twilley's Lystra Stranded Cotton**
2 skeins each of colours 2 and 6, 1 skein each of colours 69, 68, 67, 21, 15, 51 and 7.
**Twilley's White Lyscordet** (for border)
26 × 100 g balls.
11-mesh white Aida embroidery material 30 cm wide and 43 cm long/12 in wide and 17 in long. A 2.00 mm crochet hook. A size 22 tapestry needle. A length of Laura Ashley 'Oleander' cotton fabric 97 cm wide by 203 cm long/38 in wide by 80 in long (or other suitable fabric of your choice). 2.5 cm/1 in turning has been allowed all round. Matching sewing thread.

**Tension, abbreviations and Special note on Filet Crochet** – As for the Rose tablecloth on page 98.

### TO MAKE BORDER

Make 179 ch.

**1st row:** 1 tr into 4th ch from hook, 1 tr into next ch, 1 ch, miss 1 ch, 1 tr into next 3 ch, (1 ch, miss next ch, 1 tr into next ch) 79 times, 1 tr into next 2 ch, 1 ch, miss next ch, 1 tr into next 3 ch, 1 ch, miss next ch, 1 tr into last 5 ch.

**2nd row:** 3 ch (standing as 1st tr), 1 tr into next 4 tr, 1 ch, miss 1 ch, 1 tr into next tr, 1 ch, miss next tr, 1 tr into next tr, 1 tr into ch sp, 1 tr into next tr, 1 ch, miss next tr, 1 tr into next tr, (1 ch, 1 tr into next tr) 78 times, 1 tr into ch sp, 1 tr into next tr, 1 ch, miss next tr, 1 tr into next tr, 1 tr into ch sp, 1 tr into next tr, turn.

**3rd row:** 4 ch (standing as 1st tr and 1 ch sp), miss next tr, (1 tr into next tr, 1 tr into ch sp, 1 tr into next tr, 1 ch, miss next tr) twice, 1 tr into next tr, (1 ch, 1 tr into next tr) 76 times, 1 tr into ch sp, 1 tr into next tr, 1 ch, miss next tr, 1 tr into next tr, 1 tr into ch sp, 1 tr into next tr, 1 ch, 1 tr into next 4 tr, 1 tr into top of 3 ch.

**4th to 18th rows:** Work rows 4 to 18 from chart.

**19th row:** 8 ch, 1 tr into 7th ch from hook, 1 tr into next ch, 1 tr into next tr, 1 ch, miss next tr, 1 tr into next tr, 1 tr into ch sp, 1 tr into next tr, 1 ch, miss next tr, 1 tr into next tr; complete row as chart.

**20th to 34th rows:** Work rows 20 to 34 from chart.

**35th row:** 4 ch, 1 tr in 4th ch from hook, 1 tr into next tr, 1 ch, miss next tr, 1 tr into next tr, 1 tr into ch sp, 1 tr into next tr, 1 ch, miss next tr, 1 tr into next tr; complete row as chart.

Now work from chart 15 to end of 69th row. Rows 2 to 69 inclusive form pattern. Rep them until yarn is used up.

Fasten off.

Press in stages, as for the tablecloth.

**CHART 15**

KEY

Block   ✕

Space   ☐

**TO MAKE MEDALLION**

Oversew raw edges of the Aida material, as recommended on page 10. Mark centre of piece widthwise and lengthwise with running stitch in a contrast colour. Now work rose motif from chart 8. Work in cross stitch, using 6 strands of Lystra and working cross over one block of threads each way.

The arrows on the chart should coincide with the marking threads on the fabric, and each square on the chart represents one cross section of threads. Begin at centre and follow colour key. Ensure that the top stitches of crosses all lie in the same direction.

Press the finished embroidery on the wrong side, using a warm iron over a damp cloth. When dry, cut medallion into shape desired. Fold under 1 cm/½ in and tack. Place medallion face up in desired position on bedspread top fabric and hemstitch in place neatly all round.

Make double hem at top edge of fabric and stitch. Overlock other three edges. Mark centre of bottom edge of fabric and centre of top edge of crochet border. Matching markers, pin border along both long edges and bottom edge of fabric, easing in evenly all round. Topstitch border to fabric.

N.B. We recommend dry-cleaning only for this design because of possible shrinkage of fabric.

## ROSEBUD AND HEART CUSHION

**MEASUREMENTS**

Finished cushion size: 39 cm/15½ in square excluding frill.

**MATERIALS**

**Twilley's Lystra Stranded Cotton**

1 skein each of colours 67, 6, 68, 51, 7, 15, 21, 2 and 43.

A 41 cm/16 in square piece of Quick Quilt Damask with 4 embroidery areas centred on the fabric. A piece of white backing fabric the same size. A size 20 tapestry needle. 2½ metres narrow satin ribbon. A piece of Laura Ashley 'Oleander' cotton fabric 97 cm wide by 71 cm long/36 in wide by 28 in long (or other suitable fabric of your choice). Sewing thread. Cushion pad to fit.

**TO MAKE**

Oversew or overlock raw edges of damask, as recommended on page 10. Mark the centre of each of the 4 embroidery areas widthwise and lengthwise with a row of running stitches.

Now work chart 26 in top left-hand area and bottom right-hand area. Work in cross stitch using 2 strands of Lystra and working cross over one block of threads each way.

The arrows on the chart must coincide with the marking threads and each square on the chart represents one block of threads.

Begin at the centre of the motif each time, following colour key and ensuring that top stitches of crosses all lie in the same direction.

Now work chart 27 in the same way in the other 2 areas.

Press work on wrong side, using a warm iron over a damp cloth. Cut ribbon into equal lengths. Slot through as shown in the photograph, securing ends with a stitch to edges of damask.

Cut the frill fabric into 4 strips, cutting across width of the fabric. Sew strips together to form a ring. Press seams and fold in half lengthways, right side outside. Press fold. Gather up raw edges and stitch to damask, with raw edges of frill to raw edges of damask. Sew backing fabric to damask, right sides together, leaving a gap through which to insert pad. Turn cover inside out, insert pad and close seam. (See diagrams for sewing a frill on page 17.)

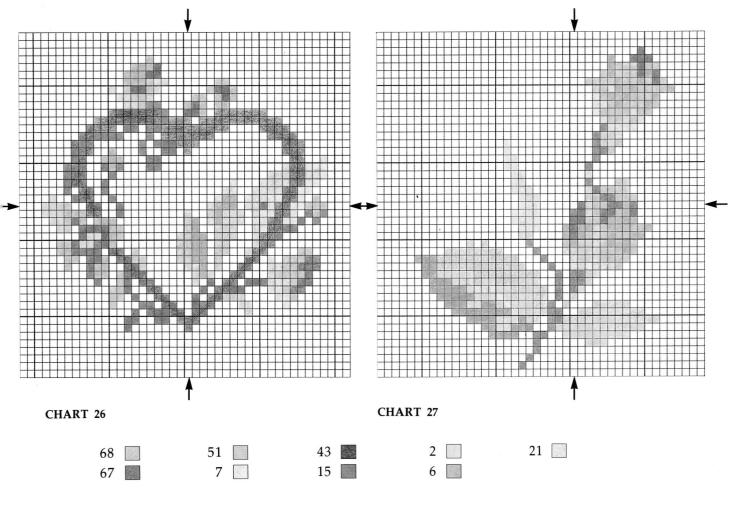

**CHART 26**

**CHART 27**

| | | | | |
|---|---|---|---|---|
| 68 ⬜ | 51 ⬜ | 43 ⬛ | 2 ⬜ | 21 ⬜ |
| 67 ⬛ | 7 ⬜ | 15 ⬛ | 6 ⬜ | |

## HEART-SHAPED PIN CUSHION

*A nimble-fingered child could even make this cross-stitch pin cushion, it is so easy and quick to do.*

**MEASUREMENTS**

Finished size of embroidery at widest point: 7 cm/ 2¾ in.

**MATERIALS**

**Twilley's Lystra Stranded Cotton**

1 skein each of colours 68, 67, 51, 7, 43, 15, 2 and 6. 14-mesh white Aida embroidery material 20 cm/ 8 in square. A size 24 tapestry needle. 20 cm/8 in backing fabric. Approx 1 metre white lace. Washable filling. Sewing thread.

**TO MAKE**

Oversew raw edges of Aida, as recommended on page 10. Mark the centre of the fabric widthwise and lengthwise with running stitch.

Now work chart 26 in cross stitch, using 2 strands of Lystra and working cross over one block of threads each way. The arrows on the chart should coincide with marking threads on fabric. Each square on the chart represents one cross section of threads. Begin at centre of the motif and follow the colour key, ensuring top stitches of crosses all lie in the same direction.

Press finished work on the wrong side, using a warm iron over a damp cloth. When dry, cut to a heart shape. Cut backing fabric to match. With right sides together, backstitch pieces together all round, leaving a gap on a straight side for stuffing. Trim seam, turn out to right side and stuff. Close gap. Sew lace all round, easing on as you go.

# PANSY RUG

## Stitched rug

---

*I was thrilled to find a vibrant watercolour by
Beatrix Potter of six pansy heads. I rearranged the
order of the flowers so that the colours balanced,
then placed them on a black background for
maximum dramatic impact. Glowing colours and a
bold design make the rug, cushion and
waste-paper basket panel most effective.*

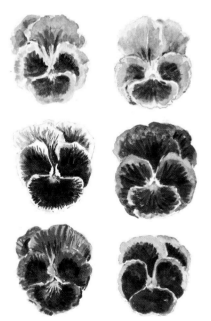

*The studies of pansy flowers were painted by Beatrix Potter
in June 1909*

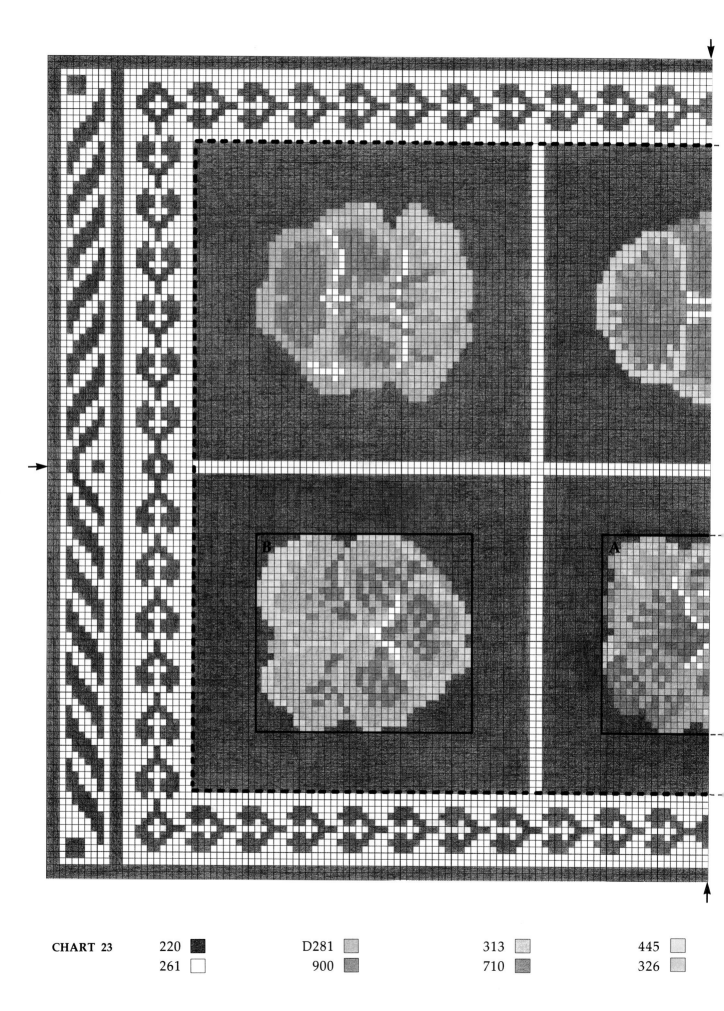

CHART 23
220 ■
261 □
D281 ▨
900 ▨
313 ▨
710 ▨
445 ▨
326 ▨

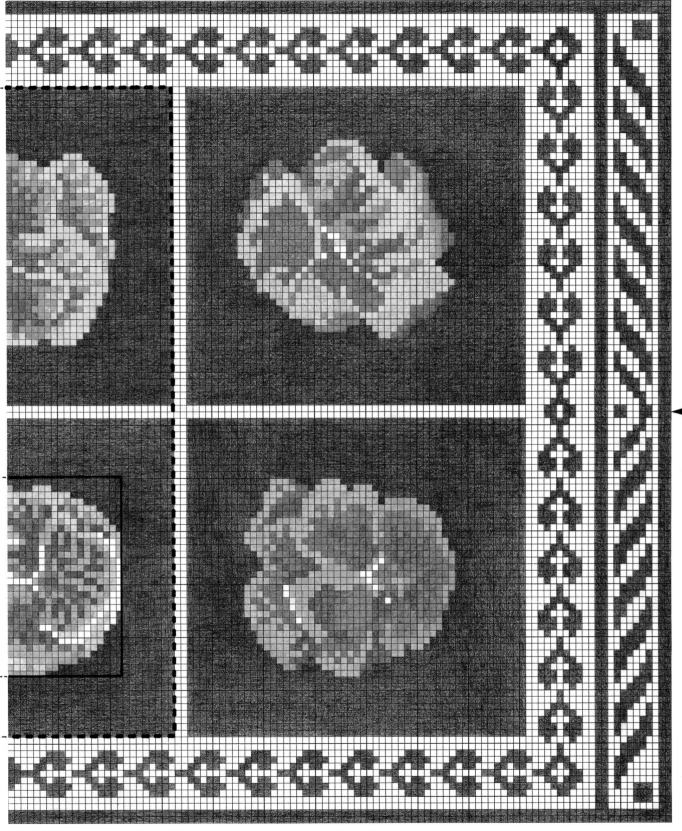

D234  ◻  320  ◻  D127  ◻  D117  ◻
910  ◻  561  ◻  724  ◻

## MEASUREMENTS

Finished rug size: 63 × 105 cm/25 × 41½ in.

## MATERIALS

**Paterna Persian Yarn**

4 oz hanks: 5 of colour 220 and 3 of colour 261.
8 yd skeins: 11 of colour D281, 6 of colours 220,
900, 313 and 710, 5 of colour 445, 4 of colours 326,
D234, 910 and 320 and 3 of colours 561, D127, 724
and D117.
5-mesh rug canvas 74 × 117 cm/29 × 46 in. A size
13 bodkin needle. Matching sewing thread. Optional carpet braid.

## TO MAKE

See the note 'Cross stitch for rugs' and diagram on
page 16.
Follow chart 23. Mark the centre of the canvas
widthwise and lengthwise with a line of basting
stitches. Each square represents one intersection of
the canvas. Work the entire canvas in cross stitch
using 6 strands of yarn together.
Trim away excess canvas, leaving about 5
squares free all round. Canvas edges may now
be lightly stitched down in place, and covered
with carpet braid over the raw edges if
desired.

## PANSY WASTE-PAPER BIN PANEL

---

## MEASUREMENTS

Finished panel size: approximately 28 cm high by
13 cm wide/11 in high by 5 in wide.

## MATERIALS

**Paterna Persian Yarn** (8 yd skeins)

6 skeins of colour 220, then 1 skein each of colours
D117, D127, 313, 561, 320, 910, 900, D234, D281,
326, 261, 710 and 445.
10-mesh single thread canvas 41 cm high by 28 cm
wide/16 in high by 11 in wide. A size 18 tapestry
needle. Piece of velvet or other suitable fabric 33 cm
high by 58 cm wide/13 in high by 23 in wide. 1½
metres/60 in braid. A 28 cm/11 in high waste-
paper bin.

## TO MAKE

Work in continental tent stitch throughout from
chart 23, following the instructions on pages 10 and
11 for preparing and blocking your canvas.
Mark the centre of the canvas widthwise with a row
of basting stitches.

Using black, work 7 rows 50 stitches wide across
centre of canvas, working from centre upwards;
now work 7 rows in same way below centre of
canvas.
Next, working above these 14 rows, work the 30
stitches and 33 rows from panel B outlined on the
chart, but working an additional 10 stitches in black
at each side. Now work 14 more rows in black at top
of pansy.
Finally, work the 30 stitches and 35 rows from panel
A on the chart, but working an additional 10 stitches
in black at each side. Now work 14 more rows in
black at bottom of pansy.

Measure the circumference of the bin, then hand
stitch the tapestry panel to the velvet so that the
tube thus formed will just slide over the bin. Cut
excess fabric and canvas from upper and lower
edges, allowing approximately 2 cm/1 in to turn in.
Turn in edges, roll back slightly and glue in place on
the bin.
Now either stitch or glue braid in position at upper
and lower edges, overlapping the braid very slightly
over the edges of the bin.

# PANSY CUSHION

**MEASUREMENTS**

Finished cushion size: approximately 41 × 38 cm/ 16 × 15 in.

**MATERIALS**

**Paterna Persian Yarn** (8 yd skeins)

8 skeins of colour 220, 6 skeins of colour 261, 2 skeins each of colours 320 and D281, then 1 skein each of colours D117, D127, 313, 561, 910, 900, D234, 326, 445, 724 and 710.

7-mesh double thread canvas 56 cm/22 in square. A size 18 tapestry needle. A piece of backing fabric

*The Pansy cushion looks most effective against dark wood*

43 × 41 cm/17 × 16 in. A cushion pad to fit. Length of braid or cord. Matching sewing thread.

**TO MAKE**

Follow the relevant area marked by the dotted black line on chart 23, using 4 strands of yarn throughout. Work the entire canvas in continental tent stitch. Follow the instructions on pages 10 and 11 for preparing your canvas and blocking it.

Mark centre widthwise and lengthwise and commence work at centre.

Finally, work 3 more rows all round in 261.

Complete as instructions given for the squirrel cushion described on page 26.

# CHECKED MOHAIR RUG

*The colours of this softly checked mohair rug tone with those of the Pansy rug and cushion: warm and rich for a cosy feel (see the photograph on page 104).*

**MEASUREMENTS**
Finished rug size: approximately 147 × 170 cm/ 58 × 67 in.

**MATERIALS**
**Patons Fashion Mohair** (50 g balls)
8 balls in Black (A), 5 balls in Wine (B), 2 balls in Purple (C), 6 balls in Tan (D) and 2 balls in Pink (E). A pair of 6 mm/No 4 needles. A large crochet hook.

**TENSION**
15 sts and 20 rows to 10 cm/4 in over stocking stitch.

**ABBREVIATIONS**
K = knit; p = purl; sts = stitches; st st = stocking st; g st = garter st; rep = repeat.

**TO MAKE**
RIGHT STRIP (make 1 only)
N.B. Twist yarns round each other when changing colours to avoid a hole.
With A, cast on 41 sts. Work 3 rows in g st.
Continue thus:
**1st row:** K, 26A, 15B.
**2nd row:** P15B, p23A, k3A.
**3rd to 14th rows:** Rep 1st and 2nd rows 6 times.
**15th row:** K, 26C, 15B.
**16th row:** P15B, p23D, k3D.
**17th row:** K, 26D, 15B.
**18th row:** P15B, p23C, k3C.
**19th to 32nd rows:** As 1st to 14th.
**33rd row:** K in D.
**34th row:** P38D, k3D.
**35th to 40th rows:** Rep 33rd and 34th rows 3 times.
**41st and 42nd rows:** In E as 33rd and 34th.
**43rd to 50th rows:** Rep 33rd and 34th rows 4 times.

Rep these 50 rows 5 times more, then 1st to 32nd rows again.
Work 3 rows in g st in A. Cast off evenly in A.

CENTRE STRIP (make 4)
With A, cast on 39 sts. Work 3 rows in g st.
Continue thus:
Working *all* sts in st st and working 24 sts in A, C or D, work as the right strip, noting therefore that first row will be: K, 24A, 15B, and second row will be: P, 15B, 24A.

LEFT STRIP (make 1 only)
With A, cast on 27 sts. Work 3 rows in g st.
Continue thus:
**1st row:** In A, k.
**2nd row:** In A, k3, p24.

*Opposite: Beatrix Potter's appreciation of a comfortable traditional interior is demonstrated in this painting of a cottage*

110

**3rd to 50th rows:** Rep the last 2 rows 24 times *but* working 12 more rows in A, then 1 row C, 2 rows D, 1 row C, 14 rows A, 8 rows D, 2 rows E, 8 rows D. Rep these 50 rows 5 times more, then 1st to 32nd rows again.

Work 3 rows in g st in A. Cast off evenly in A.

### TO WORK CHECKED EFFECT

N.B. Some of the vertical chains are deliberately worked one stitch off centre to allow for a stitch to be lost on each sewing edge.

Right strip: Begin at lower edge. Omitting g st rows at top and bottom, with *right side* facing, counting from *right-hand edge* and working into every

alternate st, crochet a chain in C on 14th st, then a chain in E on 15th st, finally a chain in C on 16th st. Now work a chain in E on 8th and 9th sts counting from *left-hand* edge.

Centre strip: Working first chain in C to be worked on 12th st from *right-hand* edge, work to match right strip.

Left strip: Work to match other strips.

### TO MAKE UP

Do not press. Using a backstitch seam (so that one whole stitch is lost on each edge) join strips together in sequence.

111

# MRS. TIGGY-WINKLE WALL HANGING

## Knitted, with embroidered highlights

---

*I love the idea of a knitted picture. Mrs. Tiggy-winkle looks very stout and homely in her apron; her features are embroidered on afterwards to make the knitting simple.*

**MEASUREMENTS**
Finished picture size, excluding loops: approximately 38 × 43 cm/15 × 17 in.

**MATERIALS**
**Patons Pure Wool DK** (50 g balls)
2 balls each of Blue and Light Brown, 1 ball of Cream, then an oddment each of Dark Grey, White, Pale Green, Emerald, Camel, Fawn, Pink and Dark Brown.
A pair of 4 mm/No 8 needles. A 3¼ mm crochet hook. A piece each of iron-on Vilene and heavyweight craft Vilene the size of finished picture. Copydex glue. 1 black sequin.

**TENSION**
Instructions are based on a standard stocking-stitch tension of 22 stitches and 30 rows to 10 cm/4 in.

**TO MAKE**
N.B. Use separate small balls for each colour area, including side borders. Do not carry colours over more than 3 stitches at a time, thus avoiding distortion of the motif. Do not knot in new colours but leave ends hanging on wrong side which can be gently tightened and darned in afterwards. Take care *not* to work tightly on upper and lower 2-colour border rows as the tensions must match tension of main part.
With Light Brown, cast on 80 stitches. Work the 116 rows from chart 28, reading odd rows knit from right to left and even rows purl from left to right. Cast off in Light Brown.
Now work 4 rounds of double crochet all round in Light Brown, then 1 round Blue, 1 round Light Brown. Fasten off.

**LOOPS (5)**
Make 8 chains in Light Brown. Work a strip in double crochet to measure 10 cm/4 in. Fasten off.

**TO COMPLETE**
Using Dark Brown split, embroider prickles. Using Dark Grey, embroider snout, mouth and claws, then outline in backstitch back of dress, petticoat, sleeve, side and lower edge of apron and iron. Using Pink, embroider flowers on dress. Sew on sequin for eye. Work a lazy daisy chain stitch around cream oval area in Blue.

Press work face down following pressing instructions on wool band, taking care to block work square first. Cut the 2 Vilenes just slightly smaller than finished picture size. Iron on Vilene to wrong side then, using Copydex, glue on craft Vilene to stiffen the picture. Sew on loops for hanging the picture.
(N.B. Dry-clean only, if cleaning is required.)

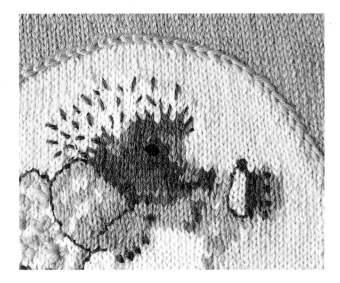

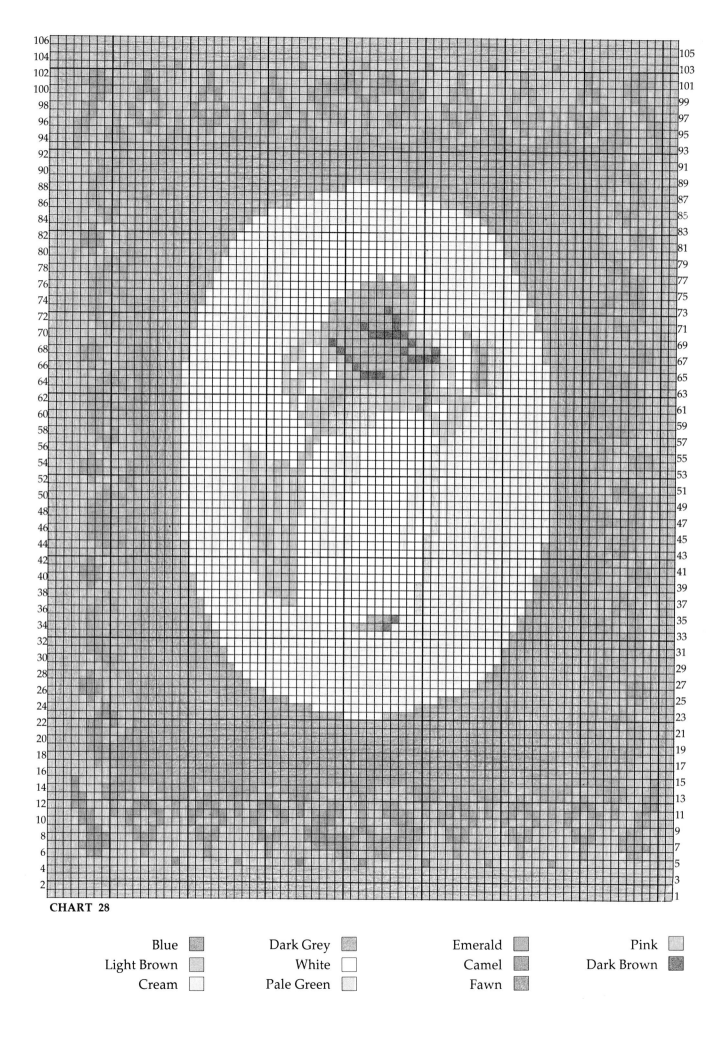

**CHART 28**

Blue □  Dark Grey □  Emerald □  Pink □
Light Brown □  White □  Camel □  Dark Brown □
Cream □  Pale Green □  Fawn □

# ROBIN CARD

## Counted cross stitch

*This delightful scene shows the little robin who found one of Peter Rabbit's shoes among the cabbages in Mr. McGregor's garden. A card to keep and cherish!*

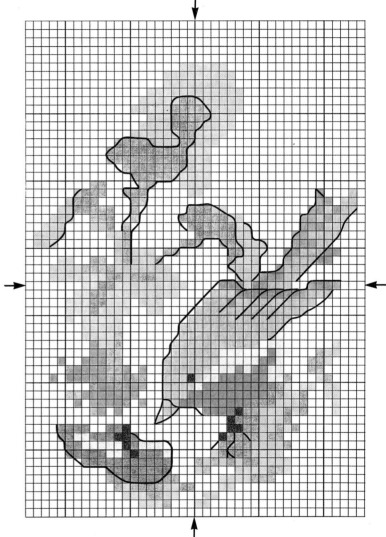

**MEASUREMENTS**

Finished embroidery size: 7 × 10 cm/3 × 4 in, excluding mount.

**MATERIALS**

**Coats Anchor Stranded Cotton**

1 skein each of colours 379, 375, 373, 2, 382, 329, 844 and 213.

14-mesh natural colour Aida embroidery material approximately 18 × 20 cm/7 × 8 in. A size 24 tapestry needle. An oval-framed card mount to fit.

**TO MAKE**

Bind fabric edges to prevent fraying, as recommended on page 10. Work a line of tacking stitches through centre of fabric widthwise and lengthwise. Using 3 strands of cotton, follow chart 24 and work in cross stitch. Each square on chart represents one cross section of threads. Begin at centre and ensure that top stitches of crosses lie in the same direction. Backstitch the highlight lines using 2 strands of colour 382.

Press with a warm iron and a damp cloth and remove tacks. Place embroidery behind the oval frame and trim to fit. Use double-sided tape to hold in position. Peel off the top of the tape and press down the front of the card.

**CHART 24**

# JEMIMA PUDDLE-DUCK CARD

## Counted cross stitch

---

**MEASUREMENTS**

Finished embroidery size: approximately 6 × 5 cm/ 2½ × 2 in, excluding mount.

**MATERIALS**

**Coats Anchor Stranded Cotton**

1 skein each of colours 233, 1, 302, 295, 266, 843, 842 and 403.

22-mesh natural colour Hardanger embroidery material approximately 20 cm/8 in square.

A size 26 tapestry needle. A circular card mount.

**TO MAKE**

Following chart 32, work as the robin card on page 115, but using 2 strands of cotton for the cross stitch. Note that a tiny french knot for ducklings' eyes

should be worked in 403 and that, if desired, both Jemima and her ducklings may be outlined with a single strand of 403 in backstitch.

*From* The Tale of Jemima Puddle-Duck

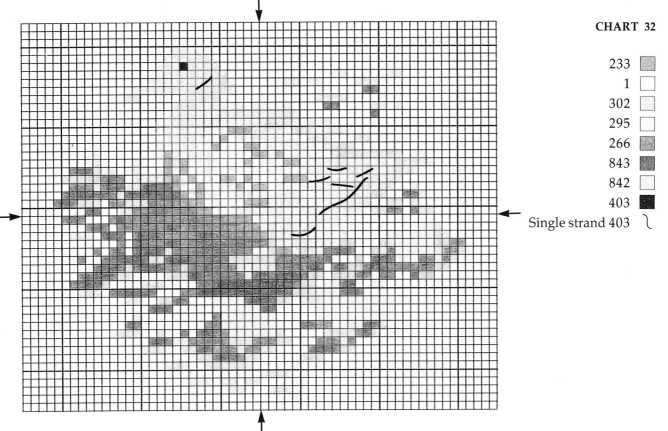

**CHART 32**

| | |
|---|---|
| 233 | ▨ |
| 1 | ☐ |
| 302 | ☐ |
| 295 | ☐ |
| 266 | ▧ |
| 843 | ▨ |
| 842 | ☐ |
| 403 | ◼ |
| Single strand 403 | ∖ |

# HEARTSEASE MINIATURE PICTURE

*This charming little picture is based on a flower study painted by Beatrix Potter when she was thirty. The watercolour shows her attention to detail and meticulous observation.*

**MEASUREMENTS**

Finished embroidery size: 14 cm high by 7 cm wide/5½ in high by 3 in wide.

**MATERIALS**

**Coats Anchor Stranded Cotton**

1 skein each of colours 890, 876, 844, 879, 107, 972, 298, 869 and 873.
14-mesh white or cream Aida embroidery material 28 × 23 cm/11 × 9 in. A size 24 tapestry needle.
Frame to fit.

**TO MAKE**

Oversew raw edges of Aida, as recommended on page 10. Mark the centre of the piece widthwise and lengthwise with running stitch in a contrast colour. Now work chart 30 in cross stitch, using 2 strands of stranded cotton and working cross over one block of threads each way. The arrows on the chart should coincide with the marking threads on the fabric, and each square represents one cross section of threads. Begin at the centre and follow colour key. Ensure that the top stitches of crosses lie in the same direction.

When the picture is finished, remove tacks. Press on wrong side, using a warm iron over a damp cloth. When it has been allowed to dry, the picture is ready for mounting.

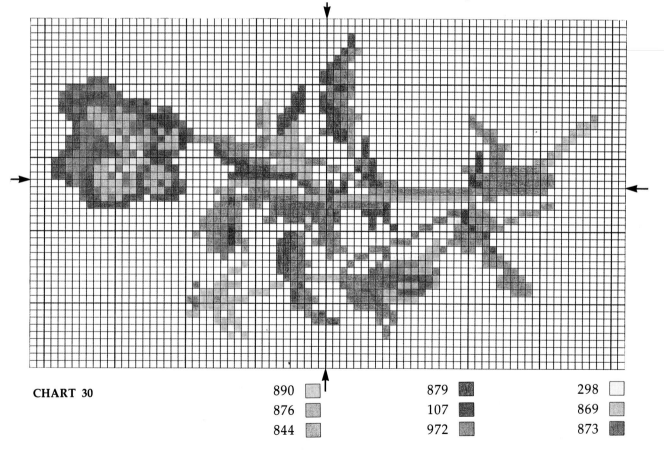

**CHART 30**

| | | | | | |
|---|---|---|---|---|---|
| 890 | | 879 | | 298 | |
| 876 | | 107 | | 869 | |
| 844 | | 972 | | 873 | |

## TULIP CUSHION

*I had wanted to use one of Beatrix Potter's paintings
of tulips but planned this cushion very much at
the last minute, after most of the other designs had
been finished. A friend showed me a beautiful old
tapestry frame, and I thought it would be attractive to
photograph it with the work still in progress.
For the background I tried to imitate the parchment
colour of the original painting; however, I think a
more dramatic effect would be achieved with a bolder
background or a stronger, subtle contrast.*

*Tulips, with their subtle colours and graceful shapes, inspired
some of Beatrix Potter's most beautiful flower paintings*

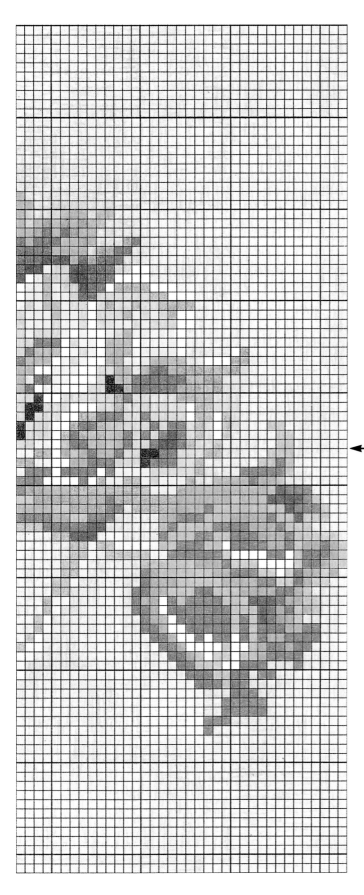

## MEASUREMENTS

Finished needlepoint size: approximately 37 × 32 cm/14½ × 12½ in.

## MATERIALS

**Anchor Tapisserie Wool**

10 skeins of colour 390, then 1 skein each of colours 608, 37, 646, 897, 3152, 10, 402, 311, 384, 278, 858, 711, 3241, 987 and 3175.

10-mesh double thread canvas 51 cm wide and 61 cm high/20 in wide and 24 in high. A size 18 tapestry needle. A piece of backing fabric 41 × 36 cm/16 × 14 in. Cushion pad to fit. Braid.

## TO MAKE

Following chart 31, work as instructions given for the squirrel cushion on page 26, noting that when chart 31 is complete a border of 17 stitches all round should be worked in 390.

## CHART 31

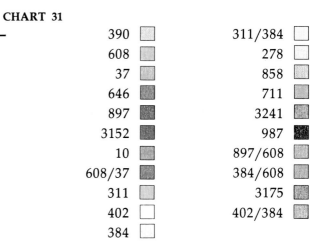

| | |
|---|---|
| 390 ☐ | 311/384 ☐ |
| 608 ▢ | 278 ☐ |
| 37 ▢ | 858 ▢ |
| 646 ▢ | 711 ▢ |
| 897 ▢ | 3241 ▢ |
| 3152 ▢ | 987 ■ |
| 10 ▢ | 897/608 ▢ |
| 608/37 ▢ | 384/608 ▢ |
| 311 ▢ | 3175 ▢ |
| 402 ☐ | 402/384 ▢ |
| 384 ☐ | |

# TABITHA TWITCHIT'S GARDEN MINIATURE PICTURE

*Here is the garden we see in* The Tale of Tom Kitten, *with Tabitha Twitchit (Tom's mother) hurrying her naughty kittens up the path to the house. In fact it is Beatrix Potter's garden at Hill Top, the farmhouse which she had bought not long before* The Tale of Tom Kitten *was written.*

**MEASUREMENTS**
Finished embroidery size: 5 × 9 cm/2¼ × 3½ in.

**MATERIALS**
**Coats Anchor Stranded Cotton**
1 skein each of colours 2, 831, 842, 843, 847, 849, 874, 883, 893, 895 and 975.
A piece of fine weight cream fabric 20 × 25 cm/8 × 10 in. A piece each of dressmakers' carbon paper and tracing paper 12 × 15 cm/4¾ × 6 in. A No 7 crewel needle. Frame and backing board to fit.

**TO MAKE**
The full-size drawing gives the complete design. Place tracing paper over full-size drawing and trace off design. With one short edge of fabric, carbon and tracing paper towards you, place the carbon face down on the fabric, then the tracing paper centrally over that and trace the design through with a pencil. Using 3 strands for french knots and 2 strands for remainder, work the embroidery following diagram and key. All parts numbered the same are worked in same colour and stitch. Work french knots last and, when working area 8, work french knots in 893 and 895 at random until area is filled.
Press lightly on wrong side with a damp cloth.

*Beatrix Potter loved to work in miniature. This tiny picture evokes the minute detail of her little book illustrations.*

1–2
2–847  } Satin Stitch
3–849

4–842
5–843  } Long and Short Stitch
6–883

7–874
8–893 and  } French Knots
895
9–975

10–831   Straight Stitch

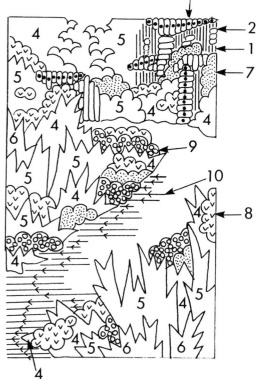

# USEFUL ADDRESSES

---

| UK | USA | AUSTRALIA |
|---|---|---|
| **Patons** | Susan Bates Inc | Coats Patons Pty Ltd |
| PO Box | 212 Middlesex Avenue | 89–91 Peters Avenue |
| Darlington | Chester | Mulgrave |
| Co Durham DL1 1YQ | Connecticut 06412 | Victoria 3170 |

| UK | USA | AUSTRALIA |
|---|---|---|
| **Coats Leisurecraft Group** | Susan Bates Inc | Coats Patons Pty Ltd |
| 39 Durham Street | (*as above*) | (*as above*) *and* |
| Glasgow G41 1BS | Coats & Clark Inc | Coats Semco |
| | 30 Patewood Drive | 8a George Street |
| | Suite 351 | Sandringham |
| | Greenville | Victoria 3191 |
| | SC 29615 | |

| UK | USA | AUSTRALIA |
|---|---|---|
| **H G Twilley Ltd** | Scott's Woollen Mill | Panda Yarns Pty Ltd |
| Roman Mill | PO Box 1204 | 314–320 Albert Street |
| Stamford | 528 Jefferson Avenue | Brunswick 3056 |
| Lincs PE9 1BG | Bristol PA | Victoria |
| | *and* | |
| | Rainbow Gallery | |
| | 13956 Victory Boulevard | |
| | Van Nuys, CA9 1401 | |

| UK | USA | AUSTRALIA |
|---|---|---|
| **Atlascraft Ltd** (*for* **Nottingham Group** *wool*) | *Refer to English address* | Coats Semco |
| Ludlow Hill Road | | PO Box 21 |
| West Bridgford | | Black Rock |
| Nottingham NG2 6HD | | Victoria 3193 |

| UK | USA | AUSTRALIA |
|---|---|---|
| **The Readicut Wool Co Ltd** | Shillcraft | Mr J F Day |
| Terry Mills | 8899 Kelso Drive | PO Box 117 |
| Ossett | Baltimore | Mitcham 3132 |
| W Yorks WF5 9SA | MD 21221 | Victoria |

| UK | USA | AUSTRALIA |
|---|---|---|
| **Paterna from Stonehouse** | Johnson Creative Arts | *Paterna Yarns are available in shops in* |
| PO Box 1 | (Paternayan Yarns) | *Australia but there is no distributor* |
| Ossett | 445 Main Street | |
| W Yorks WF5 9SA | West Townsend | |
| | MA 01474 | |

If difficulty is experienced in purchasing materials, the following addresses may be contacted. Please send a stamped addressed envelope where possible for reply. No responsibility can be taken for any materials which may become discontinued.

| CANADA | NEW ZEALAND | S. AFRICA |
|---|---|---|
| Patons & Baldwins Canada Inc<br>1001 Roselawn Avenue<br>Toronto<br>Ontario M6B 1B8 | Coats Patons (New Zealand) Ltd<br>263 Ti Rakau Drive<br>Pakuranga<br>Auckland | Unispin Holdings Ltd<br>Marketing Division<br>PO Box 38397<br>Point 4069<br>Second Floor Industries House<br>Victoria Embankment<br>Durban 4001 |
| J & P Coats (Canada) Inc<br>PO Box 5135<br>Station Street<br>Lauren<br>H4L 277 | Coats Patons (New Zealand) Ltd<br>(*as above*) | J & P Coats South Africa (Pty) Ltd<br>PO Box 347<br>1760 Randfontein<br>Transvaal |
| S R Kertzer Ltd<br>105A Winges Road<br>Woodbridge<br>Ontario L4L 6C2 | Alltex Inc Ltd<br>534 Kaikori Valley Road<br>Dunedin | Chester Mortonson<br>2nd Floor Access City<br>New Doorfontein<br>Johannesburg 2000 |
| *Refer to English address* | Coats Patons (New Zealand) Ltd<br>PO Box 51–645<br>Pakuranga<br>Auckland | *Refer to English address* |
| — | — | — |
| Kelsea Sales<br>151 Nashdene Road<br>Unit 8<br>Scarborough<br>Ontario<br>Canada M1V 2T3 | — | Embroidery Needs<br>16 Le Fueur Avenue<br>Constantia 7800<br>Cape S. Africa<br>*and*<br>Needlepoint<br>Box No 662<br>Northland 2116<br>Johannesburg |